A FAERY MERRY CHRISTMAS

AND

A READER IN FAE THEOLOGY AND FOLKLORE

Mirador Publishing
10 Greenbrook Terrace
Taunton
Somerset
TA1 1UT

A FAERY MERRY CHRISTMAS TO ONE AND ALL

A Story in The Crossover Series

By

JOHN WESTBROOK

Also by the author

The Crossover
Oh, Fae

MILLY HOPE WAS A SPRING baby – born on an uncharacteristically misty and stormy Spring day in the Middle–England village of Whimbury. Her parents, along with most other parents, had always insisted that she would be special, but in this case they barely knew the half of it.

Milly had been selected by Faery fate to be born the legendary Crossover child – a human baby who, from birth, would have the potential to cross between the Faery world and the human world as she wished. Miranda and Will Hope were not to know this, but the Faery community of the parish most certainly did. The legend had passed through the generations since the beginning of the human timescale, although few Faeries still took it seriously enough to treat it as anything more than a suitable subject for a bedtime story. Those that did, retained a faith that the environmental damage being inflicted on the world by their human neighbours could yet be reversed by co–operation with the world–wide Faery community.

The previously fractious tribal groupings amongst the Whimbury Faery community had been brought together by necessity, as the malevolent Nixies from a distant dark empire had set about trying to prevent the Crossover ritual from being completed in time for Milly to be invested into her role. Fortunately, the initiative and imagination of the local Faeries had ensured a successful ritual process and sent the numerically superior Nixies scurrying back home to a less than rapturous welcome.

Milly, of course, was not to know any of this, being only a few days old at the time. Neither did her parents, though they did notice over the following weeks and months, as Spring led to Summer, Summer to autumn, and autumn to the Christmas season, that Milly was special in ways that they had not anticipated. Yes, she was a happy and contented child. Yes, she was the celebrity of the village, which was generally aging and desperate for new blood. Yes, she was bright and picked up her motor skills quickly. Yes, she laughed a great deal and responded to a full range of physical and emotional stimuli. And yes, Miranda and Will were filled with pride as the health visitor regularly sang the praises of their daughter's development. But there were also the perplexing moments. The way she seemed to pick up signals from parts of the room where her parents were not. The way she engaged with nature, and particularly woodlice, when sat out in the garden in the late summer. And, especially, the way that she related in most animated fashion to Spot, the canine member of their near neighbours, the Potts family from the Post Office.

But what flummoxed them the most was her reaction to Spot's barking. Rather than displaying any kind of upset or distress, she merely turned her head to a jaunty 45 degree angle and adopted what could only be described as a quizzical look.

******

The Whimbury Faery community focussed around the Royal Oak – a hostelry located in the base of the tree of the same name. Barry Goodfellow, the publican, ran a well–organised establishment, and prided himself on the way that he managed to keep the warring factions apart, whilst allowing them to undertake their own amusements. The Grumplets played dominoes in the snug, whilst the Happs enjoyed more raucous entertainment in the lounge bar. This often revolved around quiz nights, with Barry and his staff supplying the questions. The louder the quiz became, the more each tribe enjoyed it – one tribe because it gave them an excuse to be seriously grumpy about the noise, and the other because they could make it.

Members from all of the seven gnome tribes were welcome at the Royal Oak, along with representatives and visitors from other Faery species. All had come together in spectacular fashion back in the Spring to thwart the best efforts of the Nixies to prevent the Crossover ceremony, and life in the village would never be quite the same again. A spirit of togetherness now underpinned the shallow façade of dislike and distaste that maintained the balance in the community. And now, once a week, all of the Faeries came together at the Inn to discuss on–going progress in the training up of Milly Hope to fulfil her role.

The legend had it that the Crossover child had to achieve the actual crossover between human and Faery before her 7th birthday. If this was not done, the full powers of the

Crossover would not be available to her, and her influence in both the human and Faery world would be significantly diminished. Already there were promising signs that Milly, still less than a year old, was responding to the promptings of the Faeries and animals of Whimbury parish into the ways of nature and of life outside of the narrow human dimension. Only when she knew and understood enough of this would she be able to take her rightful place in and across both worlds.

Barry and his bar staff, Trixie and Damien, had prepared the lounge bar for the last planning meeting before the human festival of Christmas. The Faeries had their own celebration of "King and Queen Day", coinciding with the Spring Equinox, but they appreciated the significance of Christmas to the human community, and had been working up to a major offensive on the education of Milly to take place over the festive season. And now the bar was full, as it always was on these occasions, with gnomes, pixies and sprites all preparing to work together for the greater good of Faekind.

Barry called for order and, surprisingly for such a mixed Faery gathering, got it immediately.

"Right. Straight onto updates." Barry was the natural leader since, being publican, he found out pretty much everything about everyone in the community before anyone else, including, occasionally, the individuals themselves.

"News from the dog?" he continued. "Robin?"

Robin Goodfellow, his prankster brother and partner to Trixie, was in charge of liaison with Spot the poodle. The Potts family were the most frequent visitors to Miranda and Will, and Spot was charged with establishing regular communication with Milly. Although she was some years away from being able to cross over, she already had a great capacity for communication using the verbal and non–verbal methods of animals, and the super–range frequencies of the Faeries. These gifts were imparted to her at the time of the initiation ceremony, soon after she was born.

"Very encouraging." Robin stood to address the whole assembled gathering. "Eye contact and head movements show a clear understanding of basic concepts. Hand gestures and touch show a sensitivity and empathy well beyond the normal age profile of such human infants. Spot anticipates routine conversations using a range of communication media within just a few months."

There were murmurs of approval from all quarters as he sat down again.

"Larry? Anything to add?" Barry looked down at the woodlouse standing by his feet. Larry was an indispensable member of the bar staff who, in addition to keeping the cellars and barrels clean of algae, spent much of his spare time ferreting about in the gardens and wider undergrowth of the houses and waste land around the village, listening to gossip. These positive attributes made up for the fact that he was a cockney by background and had never fully lost his dialect.

"Yers, well!" He coughed to clear his throat and antennae. "I sat wiv her in the garden a lot in the summer and inter the autumn, as yer all knows. I ain't seen quite as much of 'er since the wevver turned colder, but my agents in Over Cross View tells me that she watches 'em regular like, and always asks about me when I ain't bin able to visit as much as I would 'ave liked. But she's obviously taken a lot of what I told 'er on board and loves the insect population in the 'ouse. Luckily, the Hopes ain't too 'ouseproud, if yer gets my meanin', so we still have plenty of agents on the premises ter give progress reports." Since woodlice don't sit, he crossed his numerous legs to indicate that he had finished speaking. Those who were accustomed to his manner of speech expressed approval, while those less able to translate his message assumed that it was, therefore, a positive one.

"Well spoken." Said Barry, never one to miss the opportunity for irony when it presented itself. "And as for Robin, Trixie and myself, who have probably had the most direct contact with her, I can confirm that she is always aware of our presence and, I suspect, understands more of what we are saying than she does of what humans say to her, which invariably involves meaningless baby language and/or gurgling coochy–coo type sounds. This will, fortunately, give us a head start when it comes to the stage of longer and more complex conversations."

"When does yer think that she moight be able to start speakin' then?" Everard Gnappins, who had somewhat surprisingly managed to stay awake for the duration of the early proceedings, threw his rustic accent into the mix.

"Well," Barry pondered, "she's making a range of sounds and utterances now, so I think she will be able to speak very soon now – possibly in the next few days"

****

There are often wormholes in the fabric of space and time. By means of such phenomena, words can get diverted from their usual paths and find their way into other environments, places, peoples, times, and even universes. They can emerge as sounds or thoughts in situations never intended as the recipients, influencing the turn of events or conversations in direct or indirect ways. They are random and the exit is, therefore, unlikely to be related to the entrance. For this reason, it was nothing short of miraculous that at the very moment when many of the Faeries in the lounge bar were saying, "What was that Barry?" or "Sorry, didn't catch the last bit", Will Hope, in Over Cross Cottage, suddenly said to Miranda, "I think she will be able to speak very soon now – possibly in the next few days."

"What brought that up?" Miranda was simultaneously feeding Milly with a portion of home–made spaghetti Bolognese and wiping the wall to clear from it the globules of mince and tomato that landed there from the previous spoonful.

"What brought what up?" Will was unsure what he had just said and why. He thought he had been talking about Christmas presents.

"You said that you thought that Milly might be able to start talking in the next few days!" She made a mental note to move the table further into the middle of the room.

"Did I? Well I dare say she will. Her sounds are much more like words now and she often seems to be trying to get a particular word out – very much like 'Daddy'!"

"You're hopeful. I've never heard anything like that. 'Mummum' maybe, but definitely not 'Daddy'."

"We'll see about that. I'll bet you this bar of chocolate that her first word is Daddy!" He picked up a bar of milk chocolate from the welsh dresser and placed it in the middle of the table with a flourish.

"I don't like milk chocolate."

"Well, I'll give it to you anyway, and if you don't want it, I'll eat it for you – can't say fairer than that!"

"I suspect you probably can, but you're on anyway. Just the satisfaction of winning will be good enough for me."

"I thought I was asking you whether we had enough Christmas presents for her. I know she won't appreciate much this year, but she'll love the wrapping paper, and even if she doesn't realise it's a special day, what she gets can keep her occupied for weeks to come."

"She's got plenty! And your mum and dad and mine will no doubt bring loads more things over on the day." Miranda looked down at Milly, who was making it plain by every means at her disposal that she did not want any more spoonfuls of dinner. "But having said that, some more clothing in various shades of tomato might not go amiss!"

****

Back in the Royal Oak, Barry was summing up the conclusions arrived at in the meeting. "Right then, it's all agreed that we need to encourage the child to talk as soon as possible, to give her the best start in assimilating values from the animal world and the Faery community. So having come to that momentous decision we now need a plan to put it into effect. Any suggestions?"

"Well, first thing we needs ter do is accept that she bain't a gonna be leaving the 'ouse too much in this 'ere weather –

and if she do leave the 'ouse she'm gonna be wrapped up all tight an' warm, and covered up from 'ead ter toe in her buggy, with her mum an' dad in close attendance."

"Good point Everard! And that means of course that we won't be able to get to her that easily, or communicate other than very briefly and from a relative distance." Barry looked around for some further ideas and broke out in a cold sweat as Trevor Stout, not renowned for his speed of thought or depth of understanding, put up his hand.

"Yes, Trevor?"

"So how far away do her relatives have to be?"

Fortunately, Barry had had plenty of experience with Trevor and was able to follow his train of thought perfectly well – though in Trevor's case it was more a pedal–cycle of thought.

"It doesn't matter how far, Trevor. You are quite right to put that question, and I was silly to raise the issue in the first place." Barry had not got to where he was without an expertise in diplomacy and a measure of kindness. Trevor was totally harmless, but it didn't do to ridicule his clientele in front of the rest of the community. "Any ideas anyone, on how to reach Milly and continue her training at this meteorologically challenged time of year?"

An embarrassed silence followed, a silence borne of the experience from only last Spring the implications of coming up with a cunning plan, and the angst and tension that such a plan could bring. Barry bit his lip as Trevor once again put up his hand.

"If even her relatives can't get near her in the cold weather outside, then maybe we need to get back into the house where it's nice and warm and her relatives will be more comfortable?" Trevor's father Mack, less diplomatic than Barry and more prone to retaliate before actually being provoked (it saved a lot of time), was about to clip Trevor round the ear, when Barry spoke out.

"Trevor, you are absolutely right!"

Trevor silently mouthed an incredulous 'am I?', and smiled at his father, who used his raised hand to scratch the back of his head.

"We will have to get our messages across to her while she's still in the house." Barry paused for a moment, mentally assessing the implications of the situation. "What we need is someone who can regularly get into and out of the cottage, and whom we can trust to pass on the right information. It probably shouldn't be a Faery, because we all know what a range of unforeseen circumstances can arise when we get into close proximity with humans on their own home territory. Any suggestions?"

From his position on the floor near Barry's feet, Larry's antennae received an unprecedented input of thought–waves as several pairs of eyes simultaneously and noiselessly focussed on him. They buckled and vibrated under the strain, as Larry's legs involuntarily uncrossed themselves to support his shaking body.

"Oh no! I know what you're all finkin'. The last time I got involved in somefink like this, I got 'urled across the road by Nixies, got knee burns frew clamberin' over rough pile carpet, and got singed by Faery magic when assisting wiv a legendary rite of passage. I don't mind poppin' in every nah and then, when its easy and me mates can 'elp, but I got a feelin' that this is gonna be anuvva one of them Faery schemes what puts innocent crustaceans like me inter grave danger – or maybe just inter a grave! Nah, leave me art of it!"

"Now come on Larry." Barry would have put a gentle and calming hand on Larry's shoulder if Larry had had one. Instead he tickled Larry's chin, which was equally pointless since it was armour–plated. Nevertheless, he continued. "You know how you told me last Spring how much the escapade had brought excitement into your otherwise somewhat staid life. How much it reminded you of the Shakespearian dramas that you so enjoy?"

"Yers, but I much prefer the comedies to the tragedies, and we wasn't too far orf a tragedy then, was we? Nar be honest Bazza."

"No, I have to admit that there was an element of danger and risk in our strategy, but there's no risk this time – no warring Nixies, no intense time pressures."

"It ain't the danger and risk so much Baz, as the responsibility. We 'ad a mega–responsibility to see fings frew in the Spring, and it took it art of me, it did. I needed an 'oliday afterwards, and I still have the occasional nightmare of bein' under the control of them purple nasties. Me natural pre–disposition towards self–preservation, better known as cowardice, is telling me to keep well art of fings in future."

"I understand Larry, really I do." Barry was aware of dozens of pairs of eyes switching their united gaze from Larry to himself, as he spoke softly and pointedly to the louse alone. "But no–one is going to hold you responsible for anything. All we need is for you to go into the house on a daily basis to pass on the knowledge and advice that we give you and that the child needs to develop in the manner to which she has been born – to fulfil her destiny and unite the human and Faery communities for ever. The future of the planet as we know and love it urgently needs this."

"Ah, fanks Bazza. Well that's really eased any responsibility I might uvverwise 'ave felt about just nippin' in to the cottage for a daily chat wiv an infant human. The future of the planet rests on me, eh? So no pressure then. Why didn't yer say so before, me old mate." Larry did sarcasm better than any other louse.

"Sorry, sorry!" Barry held up his hands in acknowledgement that he may have been just a microscopically amount tactless in his description of the requirements of the job. "Yes, it is important – vitally important – that we get moving on this. We have to get her little mind thinking around all things "Natural" and "Fae" before the limitations of human understanding take hold, and now is the time to do it, before she starts talking properly. And I think you are in a unique position to do that. She loves all animals and insects, and you can relate to her like no–one else here. All you have to do is to be yourself, and pass on our Faery wisdom in the normal course of communication with her. What could be easier than that?"

"Where does yer want me ter start? There's cleaning the algae orf the barrels – that's easy. Nibblin' detritus and mossy substances – that's pretty easy too. Then there's…"

"Ok Larry, you've made your point. But will you help? It's not dangerous and we will take full responsibility, seeing as how we asked you to do it on our behalf. It's more likely to go horribly wrong if we take matters into our own hands." Barry knew, from experience that he could wear down Larry's resistance, though he would rarely play on Larry's good nature, and would only consider doing so in extreme circumstances.

"Well since you've put it so nicely, I suppose it won't hurt to give it a go. But you've got ter make it clear what it is I 'ave ter say. I don't want 'er growin'up finkin' all the wrong fings cos I messed it up."

"Larry, I love you!" Barry smiled broadly and turned to face his audience. "Larry will do it on our behalf." The pronouncement was met with loud cheers and applause. Barry allowed a reasonable display of approval and then raised his hands for silence. "But we've got to give him our total support – moral and practical. He mustn't be left to take on this responsibility alone."

"Well said. Barry, Trixie and I will certainly keep a special eye out for his welfare, and I'm sure I speak for everyone else here as well." Robin looked around the gathered masses for support and received it with a loud chorus of approval.

"Right, so let's get started on writing down what the child needs to know." Barry licked his finger and wet the tip of his crayon, ready to prepare Larry's scripts.

****

Back at Over Cross View, Miranda was spreading the icing over her Christmas cake. She was pleased with its consistency – thick enough to support a raised section in readiness for placing Father Christmas on his sleigh at the very top, poised to slide down between the candles and snow–covered fir trees.

Will had always been a traditionalist at heart and loved his Christmas cakes though, in truth, mainly the marzipan. But this year, she just knew that he would love playing with the decorations and making stories and scenes for Milly to join in. She might as well have covered a cardboard box with marzipan and icing for all Will cared about the cake itself. But she liked a heavily alcoholic fruit cake, and so did the rest of the family, so that justified her efforts.

As she applied the finishing touches, she heard sounds from the living room.

"Awake are we, poppet?" Miranda washed her hands and wandered out of the kitchen to check on Milly. She had fallen asleep in her buggy on the way back from the Potts' village shop, and so Miranda had left the child to continue her late morning baby–nap while she got on with the baking. In between residual yawns, Milly kicked her legs and gurgled happily at the sight of her mother.

"So my little treasure, let's get you out of those straps and give you a bit of freedom." Miranda gently prised Milly from the buggy and sat her down in the middle of the floor. She surrounded her with toys that could be squashed or otherwise manipulated, some of which also rattled or squeaked. Milly immediately picked her favourite tapered pole and began to take off the different–sized rings and put them back again. She appeared to be talking to herself.

"Having a conversation with yourself, are you? Perhaps daddy was right and you will start proper talking soon." Miranda tried to hold herself in check, but couldn't resist helping Milly with the rings while saying clearly "Mummum, Mummum" over and over again. "It's not the chocolate, it's the principle," she muttered to herself, and then left Milly to it when it was clear there would be no response this time.

Milly kept chattering away and crawled inelegantly over to the corner of the room, carrying a shaker ring with her. In the corner, Larry engaged her in conversation, having entered the room by his usual gap in the floorboards. He hoped and prayed Will and Miranda would not be laying fitted carpets any time soon or it would make his task much more difficult. He had already sent a few of the local woodlice and assorted domestic insects to other parts of the house to try to side–track Miranda, although on this occasion he needn't have bothered, since she was concentrating hard on finishing the Christmas baking.

Of all of the insects and crustaceans in the house, Milly responded most to Larry. Barry had always wondered if that was because Larry had been present at the Crossover initiation rites. Maybe she had been aware of him right from the beginning. Whatever the truth of the situation, Barry was glad that the louse had taken up his challenge and decided to play a leading role in Milly's training. He trusted Larry and was sure he'd put his heart and soul into it.

For several minutes, Larry opened up to Milly some of the history of the Faery kingdom – of King Oberon and Queen Titania, of the different Faery species in the village and beyond, of the gnome tribes who made up most of the Whimbury Faery community, and of Barry and the other Faeries who had played a leading role in ensuring the success of her ceremonial induction into the Crossover role. He was about to begin explaining the reason behind her significance, when he was interrupted by the arrival of Will, home for lunch from his work at Green's Agricultural Machinery workshop, across the High Street.

Will shouted to Miranda as he came in, and then went straight to the living room to see Milly.

"Hello, my princess." He picked her up and gave her a big kiss.

"No wonder human children are so confused," thought Larry. "She won't know whether she's 'poppet', treasure' or 'princess'. It's a good job Barry got this Faery training programme going when he did. She'll need a bit of security". He wandered back to his exit, and left the room to Will and Milly.

"So look who's here to have his lunch with you," said Will, and then, after a glance towards the kitchen, he continued, enunciating clearly, "It's Daddy! Daddy! Can you say that?" Despite much repetition and a little cajoling, there remained no response and, somewhat deflated, he carried Milly into the kitchen for their lunch.

****

It was Christmas Eve and Larry was back to continue his work with Milly. He had never before communicated with anything that did not have antennae – except Faeries and other insects of course, but that was different. At first he had not been clear as to how he was to get his information across, but he soon realised that humans have the potential to communicate non–verbally, though rarely, if ever, use it. Quite clearly the Crossover ritual had conferred special abilities on Milly, and she had related to Larry, Spot and the local Faeries very easily right from the beginning. Lack of human language and only a basic experience of life and nature, was but a temporary set–back. She saw well beyond her little self, and took in everything that went on around her. Making sense of it was where the animals and Faeries came in. Where human speech was unavailable, other means of conveying thought were used.

Larry explained to her the way that nature worked. It was not as complicated as humans normally made out. Basically, left to its own devices, nature sorts out how things work and interact. Animals had understood long ago where their place was in this system and acted and adapted as necessary. Humans had a worrying tendency to believe that nature existed to serve them and them alone, despite the fact that they were relatively recent on the scene.

He went on to help Milly understand how the Faeries lived. They had been around since long before humans learnt to walk upright and had a closer relationship with the world around them. They had developed extra senses and, like animals, had a wider and more pragmatic approach to living on their planet. Whilst they were prone to the same arguments and disagreements that afflicted their human co–inhabitants, they recognised that on some matters there had to be a common approach to ensure long–term survival. And one of those was to maintain balance in the environment. This did not deny the need to adapt slowly as the environment changed, but in all things, the long–term security of their planetary home was paramount.

Larry put all this as simply as he could. It was vital that Milly appreciated the basic concepts before the limitations of human understanding and language formed a barrier. Over the few days before the Christmas celebrations dominated the Hope household, he patiently picked over the points that Barry had prioritised for him and found a way to impart them to a small human infant. He was amazed at her capabilities and her capacity to relate what he said to her own limited experience of the world. She clearly was a very special child.

But tomorrow would be Christmas Day, and although Larry could not fully appreciate the reasons for the special nature of the festival, any more than he could make sense of the concept of Father Christmas, he and his Faery friends accepted the importance of the day to the Hope family. They therefore decided that, for one day only, Larry would merely observe the family at play and would not attempt to continue the training programme. Larry himself hoped that by watching the procedures and events of the day, he might gain an insight into what it meant. Maybe, just maybe, it might be a means of finding some commonality of purpose.

****

In the Royal Oak, Christmas Day was just like any other. The only day that was different was King and Queen Day, when all Faeries liked to dance and sing – partly because it was the only holiday when everyone could drop all other commitments, and partly because no–one could be sure where the King and Queen would suddenly appear, and it was best to be seen to celebrate just in case.

On this Christmas Day, Barry and his staff were grilling

Larry as to the progress he had made, and how Milly was responding. Larry, for his part, was full of positives and confirmed that he was absolutely sure that she understood everything and took it in with remarkable clarity and speed.

"I suppose the next thing is to try to make sure that when she does start to speak in human language that she doesn't say too much about us too soon. Humans have a tendency to put those who claim to talk to animals and Faeries on medication." Barry was desperately trying to work out the necessary checks and balances for the successful outworking of his scheme.

"Fortunately, it will be quite a while before she can string together groups of words and sentences, so there's little chance that she'll reveal her links with us in the near future." Robin, tried to put his brother's mind at rest knowing, as he did, how much Barry troubled himself over things that really matter and over which he had only limited control.

"True, true! But I'd still like to maintain regular updates, just to satisfy myself that we are doing all the right things at the right speed. Larry, you OK to keep an eye on her and keep feeding her as much detail as she can handle?"

"Yers boss. I'm kinda getting inter the swing ov it nar. I can't claim to 'ave intimate knowledge of the workins of the 'uman mind, but I've grown a bit fond of the little one. She's bright an' sweet, an' she don't get easily ruffled by nuffink. I was plannin' ter go back ter the cottage today and see what exactly they all get's up to on these 'ere occasions. From what I can gavver, some of her uvver relatives might be a poppin' over ter spend time wiv 'em, and it could be 'elpful to find art a bit more about the wider family maybe?

"Indeed! You've really risen to this challenge, haven't you? Don't know what we'd do without you."

"Clean art yer own cellars and khazi, I spect's. Well, I'm orf. Don't want ter miss anyfink." And Larry shuffled out of the door.

****

Miranda was busy putting the turkey into the oven and passing on instructions to her mother about roasting the potatoes and parsnips. Her mother was busy ignoring the instructions and performing the roasting procedures as she had done for the previous three decades. Will was in the living room with Miranda's dad smoking the regular Christmas present cigar that he never wanted year after year, and which was, as usual, gradually making him feel sick. Milly was sitting in the corner tearing up Christmas wrappings and chatting away to herself.

If Will or his father–in–law had been sufficiently awake and aware they might have noticed that Milly was frequently looking into the corner of the room and paying little attention to the wrapping paper as she tore it into smaller and smaller pieces.

"What time's the Queen's Speech?" Miranda's dad asked the same question every year at almost exactly the same time – to coincide with the moment when Will began to turn green and then grey, and when the conversation had long drawn to a halt. For some, and he was one of them, the Queen's Speech was the centrepiece of the day's entertainment, and it was incumbent on the females in the family to ensure that Christmas Dinner was out of the way before it came on the TV.

"Three o'clock, I think!" It was always three o'clock as Will well knew, but it gave him the opportunity to leave the room in search of the Christmas television and radio schedules. He went into the kitchen where the smell of roasting bird and vegetables, along with blanching Brussels sprouts, was marginally preferable to that of the cigar.

"How's it going?" He sat down in an attempt to get his stomach to stop churning.

"Fine." Miranda was in a life and death struggle with three courses of the Christmas meal, and winning – as she always did. "It should be ready on time and we won't miss the Queen's Speech, if that's what you're concerned about."

"Well not me, exactly. But it did crop up in the course of conversation – so I think someone else might be."

"During the course of your conversation, did you happen to notice what Milly was getting up to?"

"Not really! But she seemed quite content and sounded happy enough. Shall I go and check?" Will waited just long enough without leaping to his feet for Miranda to step in and take over the situation.

"I'll check! She wiped her hands and trotted out."

Will and his mother–in–law eyed each other up wordlessly until Miranda came back into the kitchen holding Milly in her arms and smiling from ear to ear.

"Hey everyone. Guess who's just uttered her first word?"

"By the look on your face, I suspect it wasn't 'daddy'!" Will looked disconsolate.

"Correct!" beamed Miranda.

"So it was 'mummum' then! Ho hum – I'll go and get the chocolate, shall I?"

"Neither was it 'mummum'."

"Well don't keep us in suspense, what was it?" Will could hardly contain himself.

"You're not going to believe this, and I can't explain it…" She paused for effect.

"Well?"

"It was 'Larry'! So happy Christmas Larry, whoever you are and wherever you may be."

A Reader in Fae Theology and Folklore

A companion to The Crossover Series of books.

To fully appreciate the significance of "The Crossover" and its context within both Fae and Human history, it is necessary to examine aspects of the Fae Creation Chronicles and Fae Folklore. These are complex, detailed and fascinating – at least to faeries. This compilation has been produced to sift through key elements of the vast amounts of sacred and secular writings from the Fae community in general and from the Whimbury area of Middle–England in particular.

The Fae Chronicles of History and Theology represent the earliest known writings by Fae authors regarding the creation of the Earth and its surrounding universe. In it, the role of both faeries and humans in its establishment and development are well documented. The Chronicles have been translated from the original Elven languages into human English by the Elven Languages Federation (ELF), and may be considered the most accurate of all translations. They may also, by humans, be considered to make faeries seem to be the good guys and humans the baddies. But hey – no big deal – and where does current evidence point us?

Traditional Fae Folklore would be incomplete without

reference to folk music and song. Most human folk songs are derived from earlier faery equivalents as can be seen from the selection chosen here, which would have been familiar to the faeries of Whimbury at the time of The Crossover. Faeries value their traditions and it is likely that humans will have become aware of these songs and tunes by virtue of close proximity to faeries at a sensitive time in their lives – a process not dissimilar to osmosis.

Morris Goodfellow, a travelling sprite with a home base in Whimbury, is a renowned collector of faery poetry from wherever his travels take him. The sonnets and poems reproduced here are those he collected mainly from relatively close to home, and they capture very well the cultural heritage of the faeries of this area of Middle–England. As such they help to explain the reason why "The Crossover" was enacted in Whimbury, and why the faeries of the parish were chosen to be its catalyst.

Much of the detailed background to the ritual of The Crossover, its significance and importance, is contained in the epic faery prose poem "Paradise Mislaid". The author is unknown, and it may well be that several authors were involved (see the preface notes to the 'poem'). The need for the ritual was outlined in the Chronicles of History and Theology, but the details regarding how and why it had to take place in the way it did, can only be fully ascertained from this document, which is widely accepted as having been inspired directly by Gaia Itself.

BOOK ONE
The Creation Story – from
"The Myth of the Crossover"

This extract from the Fae Chronicles covers the period subsequent to the First Beginning, which to confuse matters just a little, came sometime after the real beginning. That is if there ever was a real beginning. Some later Fae writers have begun to accept that time may be circular, in which case there are infinite beginnings depending on where in the circle one chooses to begin. Others dispute this theory on the grounds that if you were to choose the wrong point of beginning you would probably end up chasing yourself around the universe in an attempt to get born before you die.

The version selected here is the classical and almost certainly earliest version, set down by an unnamed Elven writer (or writers). Although the writing is anonymous, it is generally attributed, at least in part, to King Oberon himself, since no–one is aware of any faery beings before him, and Oberon has not chosen to dissuade any faery from this belief. Oberon has claimed a direct line of communication to the God Gaia, who reigns supreme over the Universe in general, and the Earth in particular. For this reason, it is assumed that

Oberon is eternal and that he has a good idea of what has happened throughout faery history and what will happen in the future.

Oberon's partner, Queen Titania, claims to have been around for as long as Oberon and therefore has the same knowledge but, being female, a greater understanding of the Creation story.[1] The story has no direct reference to the evolution of different genders amongst the created beings, and Oberon and Titania have frequently had heated arguments about how it came about. Faery theologians are loathe to debate this issue in too much detail for fear of upsetting one or other (or both) of them. For this reason, it is widely accepted that the story written down in the chronicles is a composite, though incomplete, product of the utterances of both Oberon and Titania. Anything else but this compromise would almost certainly have resulted in a sudden and mysterious shortage of writers in the Elven languages.[2]

This selection from the first few chapters of the chronicles takes the creation story up to the point where humans are in a relatively advanced stage of development. A more detailed account of this period and beyond is given in 'Paradise Mislaid', part of which is included separately later in this reader. This epic prose poem covers much of the content of the later chronicles but in a more poetic way, and has been included to supplement the selection that follows immediately below. It gives the back–story to The Crossover ritual and

---

[1] Which perhaps explains why Gaia is usually referred to as female in most contemporary texts.

[2] And elves have a particularly well-developed sense of self-preservation.

more practical information about the realisation of the birth and subsequent development of the Crossover child.

The Myth of the Crossover
(Adapted from
"The Fae Chronicles of History and Theology")

Chapter One – The First Beginnings

1. Before Our Beginning, was The Beginning. After The
    Beginning, there was bickering among the elements, and
    frustration amongst the Gods of the elements, because
    there was no agreement and no spirit of co–operation. In
    time, even though there was no time, there had to be a
    Second Beginning. From the place of the Gods, the
    elements were flung into infinity to find their own homes,
    each element pursued by its own God. But the elements
    were lonely in their own homes and yearned for company.
    The Gods of neighbouring elements began to meet for
    discussion, and they considered ways in which their
    elements could combine to create new matter. This
    required the disassociation of elements and then
    reassociation in different guises. Many of the early
    attempts at collaboration failed. Among the first successful
    outcomes were the creation of water and energy. But the
    Gods were tired after this activity, and later pacts and
    covenants were aimed more towards creating material for

lunch, using as a basis, as it happened, water and energy, combined with other strange items.

2.   The most inventive God was Gaia. It [3] saw beyond the food and limited self–interest, and pondered the possibilities of wider teamwork. Gaia sought a self–sustaining entity that would look to its God as creator, but would not be wholly reliant on it. That way, Gaia reasoned, it would be possible to have a bit of relaxation while the Creation got on with the day–to–day routine – not that there were any days, or indeed nights, at this time. If Gaia had had thumbs, It would have no doubt twiddled them while considering the form and extent of matter–integration necessary to put together a complete package of non–sentient bodies: bodies that could keep each company, as it were, and operate together in perfect harmony. The neighbouring Gods poured scorn on Gaia for being idealistic, but nevertheless reckoned that if Its ideas worked there might be spin–off benefits for themselves. [4]

3.   And so Gaia, having carefully considered the experiments that resulted in water and energy, searched for nearby Gods who ruled the most likely elements to be useful to Its plans. Treaties were made. No treaty was ever signed, because there was nothing to sign them on, nor was it conceivable that any God could ever be

---

[3] At this time there was no male or female in the realm of the Gods.
[4] As a result of this, a secondary Fae theology developed known as Obeism (Other Buggers' Efforts)

dishonest or untrustworthy [5]. In return for assistance with assembling packages of elements, Gaia promised to allow all other Gods to visit at any time, in order to view the resultant creation, and use relevant beneficial ideas for the development of their own schemes, without restrictions of any kind [6]. And Gaia was content, and commenced the project. This was the Third Beginning.

Chapter Two – The Universe

4.   In the Third Beginning, Gaia drew the relevant elements to itself and flung them to the six corners of their new home, which Gaia renamed 'the Universe', to distinguish it from the homes of other neighbouring Gods. The elements, in a state of frenzied confusion paired up or conjoined with other elements in close proximity. Some, for no apparent reason [7], were attracted to those with similar properties – others to seeming opposites [8]. Once conjoining had begun, it continued, with elements and groups of elements finding themselves as the literal centre of attraction. Some of the remaining independent elements or groups allowed attraction to proceed apace. Others resisted and, if consisting of enough energy, changed direction in search of destinations that would presumably be deemed more desirable.[9]

---

[5] Ah, those were the days.

[6] There were, of course, no copyright or patenting laws – nor indeed trade deals - at this time.

[7] At this stage, elements were incapable of reason.

[8] Known now by the scientific term "Elemental Contrariness".

[9] Though what they were looking for the Gods alone know – or, in fact, probably don't.

5.   In this way, there was growth and repulsion existing concurrently. The Universe of Gaia became glorious in its diversity. From its creation, there came light and heat, hardness and softness, liquid and solid and gas, colour and smell. The most attractive among the new groupings of matter continued to attract more and more free elements to its periphery, until a clear spheroid shape emerged from the confusion. At the same time, more and more elements gathered energy around themselves in order to throw themselves explosively towards the outer reaches of The Universe, in search of alternative conjunctions. So it was that spheres both attracted and repelled neighbouring spheres resulting in stand–offs, as territories were defined and the spheres circled each other as if sparring for the continuation of their very existence.

6.   And Gaia looked upon its Universe and said to Itself, "Not bad – though I say so myself" [10]. But even as It spoke, It noticed that the elements were still moving and creating new matter, or alternatively flying out to all six corners, searching, colliding and bouncing in all directions. At this point Gaia realised that It had not factored in to Its considerations any allowance for ongoing activity. In the absence of a concept of time, the possibility that a process could take on something akin to

---

[10] Obviously no-one was around at the time, so this is pure conjecture.

a life of its own, had never crossed Its mind. It had all been so easy when each of the elements was independent, and the only concern was to stop them arguing amongst themselves. Now a new framework existed, one in which simple combinations were being superseded at frightening pace by complex combinations and amalgamations. And random choices were being replaced by orderly and self–determined algorithms.

7. Gaia looked again – this time more carefully and in considered fashion. When Gods plan, they tend to think of a linear process with a fixed outcome and a constancy of response. Gaia was perhaps able to think more laterally than most of Its contemporaries, but even so, this was way beyond expectations or intent. Its universe was growing and developing within its boundaries at unprecedented speed. Obviously, being a God, Gaia could appreciate the complexities of change and the forces at work. But nevertheless, there was gap between appreciation and understanding. For the first time in its existence a God was excited. [11]

Chapter Three – The expulsion of Gaia

8. The Gods convened a meeting[12]. There was a desire to compare results and, more specifically, to have a good

---

[11] For a supposedly immutable being, the ability to experience emotion about change was a revelation.

[12] No-one knows how such a meeting was convened or indeed who initiated it. One can only suppose that there is some inherent commonality of purpose involved.

look at Gaia's Universe, so the meeting was convened for Gaia's realm. Gaia for Its part was happy to get some second and more opinions. As Gods arrived in increasing numbers, sighs of amazement and wonder became audible across The Universe. When all were present, or at least all of the known Gods, Gaia began to explain what had taken place and what appeared to be still taking place as they watched.

9. And Gaia said: "I looked at the elements and groups of elements around me and there was stillness. And nothing moved. There was no development without leadership, and so I provided the leadership by taking the elements into my hands and throwing them in all directions. Some met on the way to the boundaries of My Universe and others met on the rebound. Some were attracted and some were repelled. With some groups, the attraction was so strong that more and more elements found their way to the periphery and added to that group. In that way, the spheres that you see before you now were formed."

10. Some of the Gods began to question Gaia, saying "Why are some spheres very bright and others quite dull?" And Gaia replied "I haven't a clue[13], but I suspect it has something to do with energy." Other Gods paused and watched and asked, "what is happening on that sphere

---

[13] It is perhaps difficult to comprehend now, but at one time honesty, openness and transparency were valued principles.

there?" – pointing to a small dull, sphere that seemed alive with activity. "It's not growing, but it's changing!" Once again Gaia had to acknowledge that what was clearly happening was beyond Its current level of understanding. "It is taking on a life of its own," It admitted, "and I don't know whether to allow it or stop it!" [14]

11. And the other Gods said, "Call yourself a God, and you would let your "Universe"[15] run itself?" Gaia felt peer group pressure, but It enjoyed Its new–found feeling of excitement and was not prepared to give it up easily. "Gods", It said, "we have an obligation to explore the potential of our elements – to allow them to unroll and express themselves. We cannot just sit back and maintain the easy life with a soporific existence of non–activity." There was momentary silence. Then a God spoke up. "Who says?" came back the response. Gaia did the only thing that a God under pressure could do in such circumstances. It suggested a conference.

12. The First Deity Conference[16] had one item on the agenda. The item was "The use and abuse of elements". Gaia proposed that all elements and existing groups of

---

[14] Sometimes Gods have to make difficult decisions.

[15] This is perhaps the first known record of the use of quotation marks to express sarcasm. It is not known whether the Gods used two raised and twitching pairs of fingers to emphasise said sarcasm. Or, in fact, whether they had fingers.

[16] There is no record of a Second Deity Conference.

elements be allowed to continue to accept or repel new elements or groups in order to develop and grow. There was no seconder. Gaia was accused of endangering the Love between the Gods by setting up Its own Universe and giving elements a degree of autonomy. The new Universe was considered the antithesis of the Love between the Gods and given the name Evol. Gaia was expelled from the Conference on the basis that It could not differentiate between God and Evol. The Conference was concluded and the Gods returned to their own homes. Gaia was left to follow Its own path in isolation.

Chapter Four – The colourful sphere

13. Gaia resigned Itself to a life [17] alone with Its Universe. But it wouldn't be so bad. The Gods were pretty boring and staid and wouldn't be much company anyway. Instead, Gaia could keep Itself occupied with the ongoing activity, most of which seemed to concentrate on the spheres. Some were growing, some were shrinking; some were settled in their relationships with one another, others were rushing away from each other as if they were unwelcome relatives. For some reason, Its attention was continually drawn to the small, dull sphere, first noticed by the assembled Gods, soon after they had arrived. It watched engrossed.

14. The sphere was indeed changing, as had been pointed out to Gaia earlier. It attracted no new elements or groups,

---

[17] Presumably eternal.

but neither were any leaving. At the same time, it was definitely changing colour. Whilst it was not getting brighter, it was gaining new and more vibrant colours as Gaia continued to watch – first reds, then blues and greens. Gaia reasoned that the elements must be re–combining time and time again to create new groupings, each giving rise to a new colour or shade of colour. It was getting even more exciting.

15. Whilst It would, from time to time, glance across Its Universe, Gaia could not divert Its attention from the little sphere for long. Nothing else of any significance appeared to be happening to other spheres. Whilst each exhibited its own peculiar character, interesting and dramatic changes were not happening, and Gaia felt justified in Its decision to focus on the special, little one. The colours changed. The reds diminished while the blues and greens assumed greater importance. In addition, small parts of the sphere began to be obscured by wispy material, such that Gaia had to blow gently to move it around and improve Its visibility.

16. As Gaia peered more and more intently, It recognised that the blues and greens were comprised largely of, or even exclusively upon, water, and other forms of matter that were dependent upon water. No other sphere exhibited such expanses of water. But what was of greater interest was that much of the other matter appeared to grow in size, often changing shape, or even

nature, as it grew. Gaia's Universe [18] was not getting bigger, but it was getting more complex, and nowhere was this to be seen more clearly than on the special, not so dull, little sphere.

Chapter Five – Life

17. Gaia's attention was now firmly fixed. Nothing had prepared It for what It was to witness next. As the blue areas of water travelled around the sphere in varied configurations with the green areas of non–water, Gaia saw movement within and through them. The movement was difficult to detect. Very small groups of elements were forming in new ways, so small that Gaia had to squint to see them [19]. But they clearly had the ability to transport themselves, unaided, around the matter which surrounded them. But why? And how did they know where they wanted to go? Gaia was perplexed. It wasn't in their nature for Gods to be perplexed, and Gaia had barely had time to adjust to being excited.

18. As It continued to watch, Gaia noticed a number of the moving groups leave the water and begin to move amongst the Greenery of the non–watery parts of the Sphere. It had to continue blowing the wispy matter away, since it clouded Gaia's vision at all the most inconvenient moments. Some of the groups seemed to

---

[18] At this stage, Gaia could not bring itself to call it by the name given at the First Deity Conference.
[19] Gaia's alleged short-sightedness may be apocryphal, and may here be an example of poetic licence.

make a home for themselves in the small streams of flowing water amongst the Greenery. Other groups appeared to be content to remain away from the water. This ability to adapt to differing circumstances was of particular interest to Gaia, and seemed to It to be an indication of a growing degree of independence of the elements from their God.

19. As the moving groups scattered amongst the Greenery, in or out of the water, they became more difficult to follow. Gaia needed to use all of Its senses [20] to detect what was now happening and where. In time, it became possible to identify new forms of matter, that Gaia had never before come across. Those in the water moved differently from those in the Greenery, but never did the two appear to come into contact with each other – until a moment that would become permanently etched into the psyche of Gaia.

20. As Gaia watched and applied all of Its other senses in equal measure, It saw groups of elements emerge from the water. They had appendages that appeared to enable more sophisticated forms of movement within, on and above the water. Simultaneously, [21] similar groups

---

[20] These are similar to those now attributed to human beings on earth – sight, hearing, smell, taste and touch – along with specific God senses such as discernment, spice and bluster – the latter two of which have come to mean different things to humans over the course of their development.
[21] A meaningless term in the context of the Gods, but the only way to explain things in human terms.

emerged from the Greenery and the two sets of groups met for the first time. Some interacted in the space above the water and Greenery, others on the surface of the sphere. All of them used their appendages to move towards or away from others in a manner that Gaia found totally enchanting. It therefore called them "Enchanters". [22] This was "Our Beginning"

21. As the scene set itself out before Gaia, it appeared to be the conclusive evidence needed that this special, little sphere had become a world apart from the rest of Gaia's Universe. Nowhere else were groups of elements forming themselves into self–sufficient forms of matter that could exist and develop outside of the direct influence of its God. And Gaia was pleased that this enchanting place was both beautiful and capable of creating matter with independent thoughts and actions. Gaia did not feel threatened, but rather elated. It considered it necessary to give names to what was happening. It named all matter capable of growth and development "Life". And in a, possibly slightly reluctant, spirit of reconciliation with the other Gods, It named the process of development in Its Universe, "Evolution".

Chapter Six – Naming
22. The enchanters grew and spread. Different forms of enchanters developed according to variations, however slight, in the elements that comprised them. Their

---

[22] In human language, "Faeries".

capacity for independent thought and decision–making made them especially intriguing to Gaia, who saw in them something of Its own nature. There was a degree of intuition to the manner in which they operated, and it was obvious to Gaia that they were part of the same process that had created Its Universe, although they had taken "evolution" to a new stage. Despite the greater level of complexity to these enchanters, they exhibited a pattern of behaviour that was in complete harmony with their surroundings.

23. Gaia decided it was time to give names to the different groups of elements and matter that was being created before Its eyes, if only to make it easier to describe what was going on to any God that might conceivably pass by and look in out of curiosity. [23] However, Gaia soon discovered that it was one thing to decide to do the Godly thing and give names to its creation, and a totally different thing to work out what these names should be. There were no precedents, no Godly root terms or phrases to use as a basis. "Enchanters" had come out of Gaia's own emotions and experience, but there were too many different types of matter now around to continue to use that approach.

24. Gaia thought, and decided to throw some random sounds out into Its Universe and see what came bouncing back.

---

[23] Gaia was sure that Its fellow Gods would not be able to resist the temptation to drop in as soon as a suitable excuse could be found.

It looked at the Greenery and then yelled at the top of Its voice out beyond the spheres. A sound came back and Gaia named the Greenery 'Hutan', which comprised many 'Trees'. In a similar way, Gaia named the oceans and seas; the rivers, lakes and deserts; the mountains and valleys. Gaia suddenly realised that it was quite enjoying itself. But then it realised that there were many different types of trees, and many differently shaped and sized mountains, and many different types of rivers and lakes, with different forms of life within them. It had, therefore, to find more terms to describe the subtle variations within the main groupings already identified.

25. And so 'trees' became oak and ash and elm and chestnut and pine and spruce; rivers became streams and brooks and rivulets; valleys became vales and glens and gorges and canyons. And so it was also that the enchanters needed more names, and they became pixies and sprites and elves and gnomes and brownies and goblins. The enchanters from different parts of the sphere had their own variations, and Gaia saw them communicate with each other. Gaia thought to Itself that it would be best if It left the enchanters to give their own names to their own immediate surroundings. And languages and dialects were created. And Gaia stood back and gazed at the marvels of Its Universe. And It said to Itself, "I wonder if I should be writing all this down?"[24]

---

[24] The idea that a God could possibly be a bit forgetful is a difficult one for humans to get to grips with.

Chapter Seven – Humans

26. The enchanters lived in harmony with the rest of the sphere, understanding the commonality of origin with things both living and inanimate. They discovered, and readily acknowledged, that they were all composed from the same elements and groups of elements. From this discovery, came a realisation that it was important to talk with fellow matter as a way of promoting peaceful and mutually beneficial ways of co–existence. From this time on, the enchanters have been able to act as mediators between elements and groups of elements on issues of potential conflict and misunderstanding.

27. The relationship between the enchanters and the rest of the living part of the sphere was symbiotic and uninterrupted until a new development took place, which Gaia first noticed in a relatively isolated area of the Greenery. This development was clearly a new lifeform, though it had the semblance of "enchanter" about it. It had similar appendages, though fewer, and was not able to hover above the surface of the sphere. It could, however, move in all directions without the need for water as a medium. It appeared to be of limited intelligence, [25] though it was able to utilise other matter for its own purposes when the need arose.

---

[25] When compared with enchanters, and maybe even relatively primitive life-forms currently still in the water.

28. Using the now accepted [26] method of nomenclature, Gaia shouted into the void and there came back the word "Hominid". These hominids were generally bulkier and less enchanting than their near neighbours [27], and Gaia began to have some rather worrying, niggling feelings about the direction this new development would take. It watched as the hominids became more upright in stance and able to work out the answers to more complex problems that faced them. At first the answers relied on co–operation with the surrounding forces at play on that part of the sphere. But subsequently, things began to change, as certain of the hominids started to display evidence of frustration and impatience.

29. The hominids that seemed, at least on the face of it, to be the most advanced, and advancing, were those who set up residence in the hutan. They used the products of the trees to create implements for such activities as hunting, fishing and, latterly, provoking each other. Gaia was concerned about the ways in which frustration, impatience and competition began to set the agenda for imagination and invention. But It was committed to let these "people of the hutan" adapt to their surroundings in their own ways. In time, those that remained committed to living alongside and in collaboration with fellow matter, kept their original title, whilst those that came to believe that they were superior to other matter, were

[26] Accepted by Gaia – no other God had found the need thus far.
[27] Neighbours in "evolutionary" terms.

given the corrupted name of "Human". The emergence of the humans was the "End of the Beginnings". [28]

Chapter Eight – Earth

30. As their development proceeded apace, the humans began to diverge more and more from the people of the hutan. In doing so, they also began to lose touch with the inter–connectedness of their surroundings. Gaia watched more and more intently as the humans became increasingly inventive, until It realised that they were using only five of the available senses. This made their achievements not only remarkable, but also disappointing. That they could develop so much, whilst failing to recognise the many other building blocks that had been left at their disposal, intrigued Gaia.

31. It was not only Gaia that looked on with interest at the development of the humans. The enchanters also were paying close attention to the ways in which their, by now, much larger neighbours were exploiting the matter around them. They watched with wonder at the humans reacting to problems and issues with immediate and poorly thought–out responses. Yes, sometimes those responses were ingenious, but more often than not they simply resulted in a new set of problems. And what was more worrying was that the humans seemed to be totally oblivious to the existence of Gaia.

---

[28] Or, as it came to be known by some – "the beginning of the end"!

32. The enchanters found it hard to believe that the humans had developed from the same set of elements as themselves, and yet were unable to communicate with them. Indeed, nearly all of them seemed unable to sense the presence of the enchanters, even when they were occupying virtually the same space. [29] Occasionally, the enchanters could infiltrate the minds of a receptive human, though on such occasions it appeared to result only in those humans being hit very hard by others, or expelled from the group. The humans seemed incapable of accepting any views other than those that supported the urgent quest for growth and accumulation.

33. Whilst Gaia did not wish to intervene in the decisions made by the humans, It did sense that humans would benefit from the development of language – in just the same way as the enchanters, who had managed to work this out for themselves. Gaia convinced Itself that a little teeny–weeny bit of tinkering couldn't be wrong, and so It enabled the language of the enchanters to infiltrate the minds of the humans. It met with some resistance but, in time, the humans developed their own languages based upon the seeds planted by Gaia. This had the effect of enabling the enchanters to communicate with humans, even if the humans had no idea that this was going on.

34. As the humans developed language, so they began to give their own names to matter around them. Many of

---

[29] This was the case even before humans invented mobile phones.

the names were those already given by Gaia and the enchanters, since those terms had been implanted in their subconscious [30] from the first seeding. However, some terms needed to be added, as exploration and study increased knowledge about the sphere. The sphere itself had no name, and Gaia waited for the humans, who were the first to realise that their home was spheroid, to give it a name. With great imagination they named it after the substance that got stuck between their toes when they walked over its surface. "Earth". Gaia sat back, smiled wearily, then shook Its head in disbelief.

Chapter Nine – The Crossover

35. As the "Earth" took on more and more of its own systems, and as an increasing number of lifeforms became aware of a need to remain in harmony with those systems, so the enchanters and the hutan and the trees and other less complex organisms recognised that a constant channel of communication with Gaia was becoming urgently more necessary. [31] Gaia responded by opening up windows into Its person for use by any lifeforms willing, able and aware enough to use them. Few humans met these criteria, and those that did had often been "prompted" by the enchanters without realising it.

---

[30] The subconscious was the only part of the humans that had a degree of potential receptivity to those senses otherwise unused. It could, at times, give the humans quite a shock.

[31] The humans were far too busy pursuing their own interests to worry about such things.

36. Gaia took note of the closeness of the relationship between the enchanters and humans, even if most of the closeness was down to the wishes and enterprise of the enchanters. The enchanters came to see themselves as mediators between the undoubted abilities and intelligence of the humans, and the necessary systems that underpinned the continued health, and even the very continued existence of the sphere. [32] Many humans were, in fact, quite aware of the needs and workings of the various forms of matter and life that they were using in their development. However, they tended to be ostracised by the mass of humanity if it was perceived that they stood in the way of progress. [33]

37. Gaia saw how humans increasingly came to value power over compassion, things over beauty, and personal status over community. Gaia was worried and, in the absence of any other fellow Gods to discuss the matter with,[34] turned to the enchanters to help It consider possible ways of dealing with the situation. The dilemma was that direct and significant intervention in the methods and development of humans would run counter to the intentions and philosophy behind Gaia's Universe. On the other hand, non–intervention could be catastrophic for the Earth and the spheres beyond.

---

[32] Well someone had to do it.
[33] Not that humans had any agreed concept of what constituted progress, or how it should be measured.
[34] Not that they would have understood anything about what was going on anyway.

38. And so Gaia, reached a covenant with the enchanters that they should operate to influence humans for the common good, so far as was compatible with the need to keep the two lifeforms separate. But given their closeness in terms of evolution and general levels of understanding, the enchanters should always have the ability to create a closer link with humans if necessary. In a time of extreme crisis, that link could take the form of a human who could also be fully faery when appropriate. That human would be called "The Crossover", and the "Crossover" would have the potential to reunite the enchanters with their human neighbours. But it wouldn't be easy. [35]

---

[35] Something of an understatement as it turned out.

Faery Folksongs from Middle England

Humans have a long history of writing and performing folk songs. Faeries have an even longer history, which explains why faery folk songs have been regularly taken and adapted by humans for their own use. The humans have no idea that this is the origin of their own traditional culture and tradition, but the similarity in the tunes and the overlap of some of the stories told in musical form is incontrovertible – as you will see from the selection below.

Faery folk traditions are as many and varied as there are tribes of faeries in the different modern countries on Earth. The selection presented here are from England, and would have been familiar to the patrons of the Royal Oak Public House in Whimbury. They would also have been sung more regularly had the faeries not adopted more modern forms of cultural entertainment, such as pub quizzes and drinking to excess. [36] The modern songs sung in the Royal Oak generally seemed on the face of it a little less wholesome, though with the right

[36] Other traditions readily adopted by humans from their faery neighbours – though with greater abandon and less self-control.

mindset, the older songs were also capable of many variations of interpretation by the singers – including variations that would not have been welcome in the family home.

Whilst there are different versions of each song reproduced below, the versions selected are perhaps the most common and serve to illustrate some of the characteristics of faeries through the ages. Some are taken from historical events and others from legend. Some were made up in a drunken stupor but have, nevertheless, achieved something of a cult status in the Fae world.

Further information is given about each song and tune below, and the songs are annotated where necessary to enable a greater degree of understanding of the history and tradition underpinning each one.

ALL AROUND YOUR HAT

This is a song made popular several centuries ago by the doomsters and gloomsters of pessimistic persuasion, who were growing weary of traditionalist, nature–worshipping faeries. In an attempt to show the seamier side of nature, these singers focussed upon the magpie and its toiletry habits, as an illustration of the dangers of walking too closely in communion with the natural world. For those humans who find magpie excrement a great nuisance (especially on their car windscreens) you should ponder over its devastating impact on small unsuspecting faeries going innocently about their daily business underneath these birds, as they were going about theirs.

(Chorus) All around your hat
There are flies of every colour;
And all around your hat
There are flies of every hue:
And if anyone should ask you
The reason why it's happening;
It's all from the magpie
That passed over you.

You walk through the woodlands
And through all the fields so gay;
You watch the lambs a'gambolling,
You watch the kids at play.

Oh, Nature is a wonder and
Nature is a joy, [37]
But beware the passing magpie
And its power to annoy.

(Chorus)

You gaze to the heavens,
You stare at the azure sky,
You follow the magpies
As above your head they fly.
But Nature has its patterns
And what goes in comes out again;
The birds drop a present
On your hat like falling rain.

That's why (Chorus)

---

[37] It is assumed that this is meant to be sung with a somewhat sarcastic tone!

BLOW THE WIND SOUTHERLY

This is an old favourite, beloved of groups of male faeries towards the end of a special evening that occurred in most Inns once a week, when the inn–keeper opened a new barrel of "Innkeeper's Choice". Given that the inn–keeper was fully aware of what would be taking place that evening, the Innkeeper's Choice tended to be the barrel that had "accidentally" exceeded the regulation level of alcohol and needed getting rid of quickly. The song reflected the fear that the drinkers had of their reception once they got home in the early hours of the morning.

(Chorus) Blow the wind southerly, southerly, southerly
Blow the breeze south which is downwind from here.
Blow the wind southerly, southerly, southerly,
Leave no reminder of my pints of beer.

They told me last night there were drinks in the offing [38]
So I hurried down to the old hostelry.
I furnished myself with a pint of the special,
And before that I knew it, I'd had two or three, so

(Chorus)

---

[38] It is unclear what differentiated this night from any other night – other than the beer that would be on offer.

It is not sweet to breathe in near the hostelry
After an evening with excess of beer.
For in amongst laughter, and ribald exchanges,
There's much to expel, and malodourous I fear, so

(Chorus)

DROOPY BUNCH OF DAISIES–O

This song was the signature song of the famed faerie folk duo "Pearl and Mollusc" [39]. They gained a reputation for the theatrical presentation of their tunes, and for this one, Mollusc made a point of adding a cod piece to his costume for what he claimed to be self–preservation purposes. It was a song later adopted by the Faery Women's Movement as an anthem, and also by the Fae Florists' Guild to be sung as a cautionary tale at their annual convention. More recently it was adapted by English human folk singers to incorporate the English Rose and to cock a snook [40] at their perennial French adversaries.

1.　By the margin of the forest,
　　One pleasant evening in the month of May,
　　When all the faery songsters
　　Their many tunes did sweetly play,
　　'Twas there I spied a young sprite
　　Who seemed to be in grief or woe,
　　Conversing with her own true love
　　Concerning a Droopy Bunch of Daisies–O.

---

[39] Mollusc so named apparently after his wallet, which he found extremely difficult to open when it was his round.
[40] Human dictionaries would have you believe that "snook" is an obscure word for a type of fish. When used in the context of this phrase, however, it is likely to be much ruder and may have its origin in the fae word for the cod-piece worn by Mollusc in his musical performances.

2. Then up spake her true lover
   And took the young sprite by the hand,
   Saying, "Milly, [41] dear, be patient
   I've had to practice with the faery band.
   I searched and searched through the woodland,
   And through the gardens I did go.
   And for our anniversary,
   I picked a Bonnie Bunch of Daisies–O.

3. I took my bunch of daisies
   And laid them beside me as we played our tunes
   We played "The Mighty Oberon" *
   And practised it constantly from dawn to noon;
   I blew upon my trumpet
   Till I had no more breath to blow,
   Then at last we had a break for lunch,
   And I sat down on the Bonnie Bunch of Daisies–O.

4. She looked him fiercely in the eye
   Till he felt certain that his brain would burn.
   Then she punched him in the midriff,
   And he was sure his breath would ne'er return.
   She called him many a rude name,
   Including words he did not know,
   She said he was most miserly,
   Not to buy her a Bonnie Bunch of Daisies–O."

---

[41] Almost certainly the reason why The Crossover child was called by the same name.

5. "O Milly, dearest Milly,
   Now I kneel on bended knee.
   If I had not been out of breath,
   A charming nosegay you now would see.
   It was not saving my money,
   That made me bring this sorry show.
   I was overcome with wind fatigue,
   And I squashed your Bonnie Bunch of Daisies–O."

6. "O, lover, you are foolish,
   Though now I see you were of good intent,
   You gathered me the freshest blooms
   But through your carelessness they are all bent.
   Remember for the future;
   To the village florist you must go,
   Or you will find your own true love,
   Will be lost for a Droopy Bunch of Daisies–O."

   * Unfortunately the tune and words are lost

EARLY ONE MORNING

For reasons so deep in history that no—one actually knows the full story, there has always been a close bond between faeries and woodlice. The relationship has never been formally recognised in any pact or contract, but it is significant that at any crucial stage in the development of fae society, or at any major turning point in fae history, woodlice, or even a specific woodlouse, has been there. There are many records of such events, including, of course, the completion of the Crossover ritual itself. Some ancient authorities contend that the closeness of faeries and woodlice is due to the fact that woodlice have come to epitomise the recycling and reuse function that they play in the natural order of things, which is greatly appreciated by faeries. This old song perhaps supports this theory.

Early one morning,
Just as the sun was rising,
I heard a woodlouse singing,
In the undergrowth below.

[Chorus:]
Oh, lovely fallen tree,
Oh, tasty algae,
How could I live
If not for such decay?

Remember the fungi
That adorn the fallen branches,
And boughs that lie a–rotting
On the woodland carpet green,

[Chorus]

Oh, gay are the mosses,
And fresh are the mushrooms,
I've nibbled from detritus,
A–lying on the ground.

[Chorus]

Thus sang the crustacean,
In state of wild elation,
Recycling the nutrients
From death, decay and mould.

[Chorus]

GREENKNEES

This is a problem song, in that no–one knows the reason for the reference to Berkshire. It has been suggested that a real village is implied and that the whole phrase may be a euphemism that would only be known by locals. Ancient manuscripts refer to Greenknees as a "lust song". Modern scholars of fae folk music have expressed the belief that this is a mistranslation of the phrase used for "love song". Recent linguistic evidence, however, would tend to favour the more traditional view that lust is indeed the word meant, and that the whole song is so full of euphemisms and double entendres as to be unfit nowadays for public performance (especially the verses not reproduced here for reasons of propriety). Fortunately, of course, beauty is in the eye of the beholder, and purity of lyric in the ear of the listener.

Alas my love you do me wrong
To cast me off in this field of grain,
And I have yearnèd for you so long
Desiring to see you again.

(Chorus) Greenknees was my desire,
Greenknees my ode to joy,
I searched for you through hills and vales
To find your village in Berkshire.

My heart you've broken, my spirit split.
Oh, why did you so inflame my soul?
I only wanted to have a bit
From your basket to put on my roll.

Chorus

I have been ready at your whim
To grant your wishes and soothe your cares;
I knew my chance of success was slim
I just needed to show you my wares.

Chorus

HAL'S BAD TOE

This song is based upon an old faery legend that centres upon Robin Good, a fairy hero who is credited with inventing the modern scything technique. He is also credited with pioneering work in the development of prosthetic feet and early antiseptics. In this song he is accompanied by his young nephew Hal who is clearly not sufficiently careful to fulfil his role as hay–baler. It would appear that human adapters of this song did not understand the fae lyrics and came up with their nearest equivalent, which was, of course, Hal n Tow, which may or may not mean "pull the rope". In any event, the human lyrics make no sense whatsoever in the context of the title, and may have been made up on the spot by translators using words of similar general sound but no meaning when put together. The fae version is self– explanatory.

Take the scythe and swing the blade,
Tis sharpened till it gleams as new:
Your father's father swung it
And your father swung it too

Robin Good* and Little Hal
They've both gone to the fields–o,
Where Hal trips over Robin's blade
And raises up a weal–o.

(CHORUS) Hal's bad toe, watch the swelling grow.
it shines bright, red as any rosy–o
It welcomes in the summertime
It welcomes in the hay–o,
Tis brighter than the harvest moon
that guides us on our way.

What happened to the hay bales
That feed our cows and sheep–o?
Well, they're not getting parcelled up,
Cos Hal has fell asleep–o.

(CHORUS)

God bless Hal's foot and toesies
Which he hides out of sight–o;
His swelling keeps him in his bed,
It throbs by day and night–o.

(CHORUS)

* An ancestor of Robin Goodfellow

LITTLE SIR PUGH

This song was a favourite of another famous fae folk duo – Frogeye and Spawn. They were a father and son duo. The father, whose real name is now lost in the annals of time, was renowned for having eyes set very high up his head – hence the nickname that stuck throughout his professional career. The song itself was popular amongst the more left–wing of the fae community, who saw it as a warning to privileged elves who were brought up to have an inflated view of their own worth and significance. Whilst it may have been based upon a true story, it is seen as a symbol of the rising up of the working–class faeries against their self–serving and narcissistic employers and supposed betters. It is likely that the human version (Little Sir Hugh), whilst more gory, exhibits a tangential reference to the same theme, and why it has become popular again in recent years. It begs the question "who is Hugh?"

(Chorus:) Mother, mother make my tea
Get me scones with jam and cream
Bring me fruit with a silver spoon
That mirrors my esteem.

Four and twenty bonny village boys playing on the Green,
Along came little Sir Pugh, intending to be mean,
He kicked their ball so very high, he kicked it up a tree

He laughed and laughed, and mocked them all, no gentle playmate he.

Out came his nanny Gay, calling out his name;
"Come in, come in little Sir Pugh, finish now your game."
"I won't come in, I shan't come in, I'm playing with my friends.
I'm having fun, and you're no–one to tell me when it ends."

Chorus

Out came his mother's maid, out came his nurse;
Out came the cook and her boy, they all did swear and curse.
"Come in, come in little Sir Pugh, your tea is getting cold".
"I won't come in, by likes of you I never shall be told."

Chorus

The maid, the cook, the nurse and the boy, looked each other in the eyes,
They picked him up and carried him home, ignoring all his cries.
The village boys they laughed and laughed, they mocked him as he screamed,
And never more was little Sir Pugh in their eyes esteemed.

Chorus

SOGGY SOGGY SUE

This song has been based on a real faery, who achieved celebrity status by being the first female faery farmer to cultivate watercress as a commercial crop. She had to overcome much suspicion from the wider farming community who were convinced that watercress would never provide a decent living for a sole farmer. As a point of principle, and because she was stubborn and bad–tempered, she worked alone for the early years of her career. Apparently, when she turned up at Whimbury in saturated clothing, but with a very substantial crop of cress, the rest of the village were grudgingly respectful and the term Soggy, Soggy Sue was one born of good humour. The good humour must have been reciprocated because no–one is quite sure how she managed to end up with a son, particularly given her pre–disposition to turning up at village functions with river weed and algae in her clothing and elsewhere about her body. In later compilations of folk songs from the area she became known as "The Water–Daughter" and several folk troupes named themselves after her or her son.

When I was a young girl I lived all alone
And I had my own small farm
I lived a life of solitude,
And never did no harm

I donned my boots one harvest time

And to the stream did go,
Twas there I picked my watercress
But fell into the flow.

I took my cress to Whimbury Fair
Full sodden as the dew,
The village folk all laughed at me
And called me Soggy Soggy Sue.

I wept, I cried, I tore my hair
But ah, what could I do,
From that day on when at the Fair
I've been known as Soggy Soggy Sue.

And now I'm old and I live with my son
He works both hard and true;
I look on him with a mother's pride
For he is Soggy Soggy too.

THE ROYAL OAK

This song is based upon another true story, this time of a group of ramblers who got lost in the hills of Middle England. They set off initially to follow a pilgrims' route from the borders of Wales to the holy Monastery of Whimbury Dale. The monastery was dedicated to St Malt, who almost certainly never existed, but became the patron saint of drinkers. Then, as tradition was superimposed onto tradition, the monastery set up a distillery, which turned it into a popular place of pilgrimage. The leader of the expedition celebrated in this song was a "holy" man of good intent but negligible skills in the leadership and orienteering departments. His mutinous co–ramblers were desperate for a drink and so left him to fend for himself. No–one knows what became of him, though rumours of a hermit setting up in a cave in the area soon afterwards may offer some clues. The story was radically changed by human songsters, who used the decimation of the oak forests of the south of England for the creation of strong fighting ships as a better use of the tune with the same name.

As we were walking through hills and vales,
We'd not been gone weeks but two or three,
Afar we saw the Royal Oak,
A welcome sign to such as we.

We had to cross a river deep:
And climb a hill, with rucksacks full.
The path was rough, the way grew dark,
We wrapped ourselves in English wool.

We slept all night, we woke at dawn,
The birds did sing, the woods were still,
<u>We asked our leader, which way to walk;</u>
<u>He said "It's just over yonder hill"</u>

Our leader was a valiant man,
He could boldly fight, but not read a map:
We climbed three hills and down again,
But if we complained we got a slap.

We'd had no ale since we left home,
Our hearts were weary, our voices croaked:
And as the sun began to set.
Still we could not see the Royal Oak.

That night we stole our leader's compass.
And used the stars to guide our way,
Until we reached our destination,
And stepped inside to spend the day.

We ordered drinks to tide us over,
They came in glasses, eight, nine, ten.
Oh five we drank, and five we spilt,
And then we started over again.

If anyone then should enquire
As to our gallant leaders's fate,
We'll toast his health in faery ale
And in the Royal Oak we'll sit and wait.

THE WHIMBURY POACHED EGG

This version of the song was first presented at the Whimbury Fair Convention, where it became the theme song. The earlier somewhat raw version was modified and "cleaned up" by the resident folk group, who adopted the name of the event and became one of the most popular folk bands of the time. Apparently poached eggs were the accepted delicacy of the great and the good at the Convention, which was dedicated to food and farming matters. As years passed, it also took on the form of a music festival and was held at the time of harvest when the crops were ready.

When I was chef's apprentice at the famous Whimbury Arms [42],
Full well I served my master with nary an alarm,
He taught me how to bake and roast with all their many charms,
Oh, 'twas my delight on a Friday night to wipe my floury palms.

I learnt to cook a Strong'n'off with pasta or with rice,
I was complimented daily for my leek and onion pies
And when I burnt the rhubarb tart, the chef gave me advice

---

[42] This song probably dates back to when the Whimbury Arms (later converted to a fae care home) served wholesome food at lunchtimes and in the evenings

Oh, 'twas my delight on a Friday night to offer chunky fries[43]

And as the patrons tried their best to empty every keg
I'd tempt them all with jellied peel and vegetable "frog's" leg
But no matter what the special was, the customers would beg,
Oh, 'twas my delight on a Friday night to poach them all an egg.

They didn't want them scrambled and they didn't want them fried
They wouldn't let me boil an egg, no matter how I tried;
They followed a tradition dear – it had to be applied
Oh, 'twas my delight on a Friday night to poach whate'er betide.

So here's to all the gentlefolk who to the chef did call
Not for a roast, or beans on toast, or puddings large or small,
But for the produce of the hen, the duck, the goose or quall [44]
Oh, 'twas my delight on a Friday night to poach an egg for all.

---

[43] It is believed that the Whimbury Arms was the first Fae establishment to feature such a side dish on its menu
[44] The ancient Fae word for quail

WHIMBURY FAIR

This is a joyful, if somewhat poignant, dedication to the traditional faery country fairs with their food stalls, craft stands and drinks marquees. In this case, Whimbury Fair was one of the more famous of its type and attracted fae folk from miles around. In the case of the younger faeries, it was an excuse to meet up with the females of the parish on neutral territory. Unfortunately, more often than not, the females were involved in the craft stalls and creative side of the Fair, whilst the males tended to congregate in the drinks marquee. As a result, there was more in the way of missed opportunity than budding romance, as the drinking often lasted till after the craft stallholders had left. The males then had no option but to drown their sorrows. Plus ca change!

We're all going to Whimbury Fair
Pasties, pies and Innkeeper's Choice;
We'll eat and drink till we've had our fill,
Then we'll make a very rude noise.

There I will buy me a cambric shirt,
Pasties, pies and Innkeeper's Choice;
With leggings and socks in fine needlepoint
And a fancy string belt to give me some poise.

There's knick–knacks a–plenty and fine antiques too,
Pasties, pies and Innkeeper's Choice;
Ceramics and pots and candles and spoons,
And for the children some half–broken toys.

While I am there I will search for my love,
Pasties, pies and Innkeeper's Choice;
She's selling her wares at the bric–a–brac stall,
But if she's gone home, I'll stay with the boys.

We're all going to Whimbury Fair,
We'll sing songs till we have no voice,
We'll toast our loves, ourselves and our friends,
With pasties, pies and Innkeeper's Choice.

WILD MUTTON TIME

This humorous ditty was introduced to the canon of traditional faery folk songs by the famous family of metal–workers who came to be known as the Copper–pots. They suggested that the story was taken from an old family tale about how the children used to amuse themselves totally harmlessly in the good old days by spiriting away sheep from the flock and worrying human shepherds almost to death, by virtue of thinking they had lost some of their only valuable possessions. True, no harm ever came to the sheep, but some shepherds who had suffered from the prank were reported as having spent the rest of their lives repeating Yan, Tan, Tethera over and over to themselves, while rocking violently on their chairs on the porch and whittling their crooks into sharp javelins.

O the summer time has come
And the trees are gently swaying,
The sheep are in the fields
With their lambs a–sweetly playing
Shall we go Laddie go?
To cause a bit of bother
Tis the wild mutton time
See them roam around the heather
Shall we go Laddie go?

I will go with my best friend
To steal a sheep and lamb–o
Tis the wild mutton time
But we must beware the ram–o
Shall we go Laddie go?
To cause a bit of bother
Tis the wild mutton time
See them roam around the heather
Shall we go Laddie go?

If we hide the sheep and lamb
Where the shepherd cannot see them,
He will count, then go and search,
But we will later free them.
Shall we go Laddie go?
To cause a bit of bother
Tis the wild mutton time
See them roam around the heather
Shall we go Laddie go?

And when the shepherd he returns
Desirous of his bed–o,
He will count and count again
And he will scratch his head–o.
Shall we go Laddie go?
To cause a bit of bother
Tis the wild mutton time
See them roam around the heather
Shall we go Laddie go?

SONNETS AND POEMS FROM THE COLLECTION OF MORRIS GOODFELLOW

Morris Goodfellow is an itinerant sprite who has travelled extensively, partly because he never felt able to settle down in one place for any length of time, and partly because he believed that if he kept moving, it would be more difficult for anyone to track him down. Morris is the brother of arch–japester Robin Goodfellow – known as Puck to his friends, and other things to those not counted as such. That makes him also the brother of Barry Goodfellow, sometime publican at the Royal Oak in Whimbury. It was on a rare journey home that Morris, along with Robin and Barry, fell accidentally into the middle of the Crossover Ritual in Whimbury.

After the conclusion of the Crossover episode, Morris reverted to his travels and is credited with spreading tales of that great adventure far and wide. The importance of this cannot be overstated, since faeries in general have a mistrust of written tales, unless there is someone around who can verify that they have subsequently achieved authenticity through word of mouth originating with an eye–witness. The theory goes that anyone could write something down and claim it to be true, but only if someone had taken the trouble to learn the story and then had the belief and patience to repeat it many times over for no obvious reward, could it be considered true history.

Furthermore, in many faery cultures, stories and poems were currency and travellers would only repeat theirs in exchange for someone else's. It may be assumed therefore that the extensive portfolio of Morris's poems and stories is, at least in part, payment for his first–hand stories of the Crossover child.

In the collection below, which is only a small part of the overall folio, the origins of the poems and sonnets are given where they are known and remembered by Morris. They have been selected to shed a little more light on the loves, travels, beliefs and cultures of faeries who live or have lived close to Whimbury. There are many others, gathered from near and far that will have to wait for another opportunity to be aired in public at a later date.

AS I DID TRAVEL

Morris came across this poem when sharing a boat across the Bristol Channel with a fellow traveller named Keith. Keith had been to lands that Morris had never even heard of [45] and had written many stories and poems about his travels. Morris was particularly struck with this poem and wrote it down to read again at a later date [46]. It seemed to him to offer hope for the future, to be found in the kindness and experiences of others, wherever they lived or originated.

As I did travel far across the sea
So many kindly faeries I did meet,
And all of them with outstretched hands did greet,
To welcome someone new and strange as me.
From islands floating in an azure sea
To mountains drawing me towards the sky
I watched as dreams of poets stole my eye,
And felt as near to God as I could be.
Then as I heard the tales of far–off lands
From strangers who had taken me to heart,
My narrow mind began to understand
That neither they nor I had been apart.

---

[45] Which, since Morris had travelled the sphere extensively, made him just the tiniest bit suspicious of the veracity of Keith's stories. Not that he cared, because they were good ones and deserved to be true.

[46] When he was less seasick – Morris preferred travelling overland.

I tore the sterile future of my plans
And vowed that I would make a brand new start.

A FAERY'S STORY

Whilst all of the poems in this selection express something of the life and culture of the fae community, this is one of the few that display the full awe and respect that faeries have for King Oberon and Queen Titania – the only royalty they have ever known. It would appear that Oberon and Titania have always been benign and caring, otherwise this poem might have been written differently. It is attributed by Morris to a writer he met in Stratford upon Avon.

Over mountain, over river,
Under bramble, under roots
Through the snow that makes me shiver,
Past the bush with summer fruits.
I run and run throughout the seasons
Upon the errand of my king,
And I need not ask the reason,
It is enough that I should bring
The flowers that give him joy and cheer;
And wake him with their fragrant nose,
Snowdrops of the infant year,
Followed by the summer rose
My aim to serve, and serve unseen,
The better for my King and Queen.

NO FAERY IS ALONE

Fae life is dependent upon teamwork. Most faeries have an innate sense of the need to work with and for one another. This poem by "John the Thinker" [47] epitomises this interdependence, and is apparently influenced by his observations of the workings of his drinking companions at the Royal Oak in Whimbury, where he lived a short while before the Crossover event. The end of the evening in the Lounge Bar tended to be a raucous affair and John wrote this to emphasise the need for every faery to watch each other's back, and for at least one in the group to have a sense of time. He was also renowned for his tendency to shout out "John's Done" whenever he finished a poem.

No faery is alone, [48]
Or lives in isolation,
Each has its place upon the sphere
That connects with every other.
If one is missed from close–knit team,
The body corporate suffers
And is diminished by the loss.

---

[47] Better known by some as John the Drinker, though he maintained his occasional comatose state was entirely due to meditation and/or composition.

[48] Except for the occasional hermit, although even these are usually visited regularly by their mothers to bring them a packed lunch and clean underwear.

The line is shortened at the bar

And the list is incomplete.

The faery with untimely earthly needs,

Will lose its place.

And so, be ready for the bell that is rung three times,

It means last orders.

SPRING WILL COME

This is one of the few poems collected by Morris that was almost certainly written by a female faery. It wasn't that female faery poets were unwelcome or unappreciated, merely that, at the time, most female faeries felt fulfilled by other forms of creativity, including farming, manufacturing and, of course, running the family. [49] But this poem clearly identifies the understanding of female faeries with regard to the place of fae culture and tradition in the complex order of nature and evolution. Morris says that he picked up the poem from relatively far away in the Valley of the Tees, though it may even have originated from much further afield. Either way, it is now a firm favourite of faeries, male and female, across Middle England.

Spring will come, with sight and sound
Of life emerging from the ground.
Birds will sing and frogs will croak,
And buds appear upon the oak:
The crocus and the snowdrop both
Will mark the end of winter's sloth,
And we will rise and watch the dawn

---

[49] As a truly matriarchal society, females largely decided for themselves what their role would be in the community. On her rare personal appearances, Titania could often be seen winking at nearby female faeries whilst nodding knowingly in the direction of Oberon, and making appropriate hand gestures.

Awaiting kit and cub and fawn;
And they in turn will seek us out
To play with trust and faith devout,
The Earth to us will ever be
A place of complex harmony.

HOW SHALL I COMPARE YOU

There is a mildly romantic side to Morris that few are privileged to witness. Behind the rugged, adventurer, "who–cares", exterior, lies a rugged, adventurer, "I–care" heart. Whilst he likes nothing more than to visit new places and meet new people, every once in a while he has a yearning for his base and the people that mean most to him. No–one knows if he has ever had that one special person, but there have been suspicions, (and sniggers and finger pointing), around Whimbury from time to time. Despite his interest in poetry as a cultural phenomenon, he has never really been one for deep, romantic stuff, which probably explains his simple, no–nonsense approach to relationships, as expressed in this sonnet, collected again from a source in Stratford upon Avon.

How shall I compare you, or shall I
Not try to bind you with the ties of words.
For in our words, no matter how I try,
There is not one that would not sound absurd.
To liken you to summer in its prime
Would be to miss the risk of stroke of sun; [50]
While spring, when at its best, can be a time
Of beauty and a freshness just begun,
When at its worst, is time of storm and wind.
The autumn has its colour it is true;

---

[50] We, of course, would now call this sunstroke.

But also has its mists, and close behind
Is winter, with its ice and snowstorms too.
And so, I do not try to liken you:
Just like and love and welcome you anew.

THE HAWK

Morris always had a fascination for faery myths, stories and legend from the Celtic period [51]. In particular, he remains fascinated by the belief that Hawks and Falcons are messengers between the living and the dead, crossing 'spiritual' barriers and transcending time. This was emphasised by the frisson of fear that faeries had, that such raptors could therefore whisk them away in an unguarded moment, hence the fae phrase for disappearance – 'Unwrapped by a raptor'. This sonnet was written by a member of the Hop family, famed for his macho nature and lack of fear of hawks. [52]

I saw this morning flying o'er the heath,

Above the gorse and bracken that form the carpet beneath,

A hawk in all its pomp and glory, which did its majesty bequeath

To all the sky around, and in its beak a wreath,

Of talon–torn grasses and thorns sharp as lions' teeth –

A wrapping for its prey entombed within a sheath;

A Celtic symbol understood from Leith to Meath and Neath.

---

[51] Fae historical periods mirror those of their human counterparts – or, more strictly, vice versa.

[52] And, apparently, lack of fear of deviating from the established metre and rules for sonnets!

With beauty, strength and honour, it passes through the veil,
And takes the spirit to a pasture new,
A field Elysian that cannot fail
To quench the thirst of travellers with its dew;
And beyond, across the wide Okeanos sail,
Until the light of paradise shines through. [53]

---

[53] This poem was obviously written after Paradise had first been mislaid and then rediscovered.

WHIMBURY GREEN

One night in the Royal Oak, Morris got talking to a poet who, though now travelling, was spending his later years chiefly in the north of England. Fortified by a glass or two [54] of Barry Goodfellow's Innkeepers Choice, he confessed that, while he loved his native Fells and Lakes, he had been surprised by the more modest beauty of the traditional village green in the centre of Whimbury – what he called 'the most perfect example of such a feature that he had ever come across'. Although his tendency had been to write about wild flowers and bulbs, he felt moved to pen a poem especially for Whimbury Green when he returned home. This he did, and sent this copy to Morris for his collection.

In all the Earth there is no view so fine:
No sight for weary eyes, nor village scene,
That can compare to that of Whimbury Green:
The daisies fair and chamomile, like wine,
Caress the nose with notes of summer fruit;
And round the Green, the shelter of the trees,
Protection for the Fae from rasping breeze;
The owls on lofty branch don't give a hoot.
Never did the earth and sky combine,
To paint a picture, splendid in all ways,
As nature from its palette can define

---

[54] Or three.

No limits to its splendour, and no greys
Can dull the blaze of colour I call mine
To own, and claim the music that it plays.

SPRITES

This poem was written by Morris himself on one of his visits home to Whimbury. He claims to have adapted it from another poem – about nature – that he picked up on his travels in North America, but which he considered to be somewhat twee and 'Birthday Cardy'. Morris wasn't known for his literary prowess, but he did know a lot about Sprites and was proud of his heritage. The poem celebrates the role of Sprites within the Fae community of Whimbury. Two copies hang in the Royal Oak above the bar – one a framed and signed copy, and the other full of small holes where the annual pub darts competition got a little out of hand. [55]

I think that I could never write
A poem lively as a Sprite:
A Sprite who ever loves to jest
And put its fellow fae to test:
A Sprite that's full of pranks and japes
Of cunning plans and wild escapes.
Of charm and boundless energy
That permeates all Whimbury.
A Sprite is born to laugh and joke,

---

[55] There is disagreement over whether the desecration of the poem was due to an excess of gnome/sprite rivalry, or to an excess of Innkeepers Choice. Either explanation fails adequately to take into account the fact that the area above the bar is a long way from the dartboard.

And spread joy through the Royal Oak:

A Sprite believes that it is good,

To liven up the neighbourhood.

DOZY MAN BAZ

This is the only extant example of a poem dictated to a Fae scribe by a woodlouse. The woodlouse was an ancestor of Larry the louse, who later, of course, became an invaluable 'backroom' [56] *member of the staff at the Royal Oak. This highly literate ancestor* [57] *is credited with inspiring Larry to pursue his research into the classical theatre of both human and fae communities. The poem was written at a time when Barry Goodfellow had just taken over as publican at the Royal Oak and was still finding his feet. His early attempts to turn the Royal Oak into a gastrognomic phenomenon were not altogether successful, and he was often mocked, unfairly, for his efforts.*

I met a man who stood behind a bar
Who told me of the travails of his role;
He said "I dedicate my heart and soul
To serving faery folk from near and far.
I will provide them with the widest choice
Of ales and food from natural goodness made.
I have my culinary skills displayed."
He went on to describe his many ploys
For weaning hardened faefolk to his fare.
I thought him optimistic in extreme.

---

[56] Technically, a "Cellar" member.
[57] Known as "Shelly" because he often had to roll up into his armoured ball to avoid being crushed at throwing-out time

But to broaden their horizons was his dream,
And he showed me one small dish he had prepared.
"My first attempt," he said, "It's true, did fail,
But Ramekin the Second will prevail."

DO NOT LET THE NIGHT

Morris was allowed to use this poem – by a Welsh poet – as a rallying cry to faeries everywhere (and especially, of course, in Whimbury) not to allow the principles and processes of Gaia to be overthrown unopposed. The poem was translated for him from the Welsh language, with the exception of the Latin phrase "Carpe Diem", which was the original title of the poem and was left intact in line three. When Morris first attempted to read the poem in the Royal Oak he only got as far as the title before being booed off and having dominoes thrown at him. [58] From then on, the English version was used.

Do not let the night creep up on you
As one who leaves the future to her fate.
Seize, seize the day, that fades from view
Unless it be compelled instead to wait
Until the remnant of the light is put to use
For goodness over darkness to prevail.
Delay not, nor be caught in light diffuse,
See, see what work for justice may entail,
And follow to the end your guiding star.
Do not be deaf to hearing nature call
But be an advocate drawn to the bar
Of mediation, in cause of Gaia standing tall.

[58] The severity of the uprising can be judged by the fact that the dominoes were in use in a game at the time. Faeries do not take kindly to the use of what they see as pompous language in a pub.

Let righteous anger see the light of day
And focus it against the evil few
Who over faery homes seek to hold sway.
Do not let the night creep up on you.

WHEN

This poem, by a member of one of the Kipper tribes living near Whimbury, has become something of an anthem for the Fae community in general. It describes an aspiration for positivity to underpin the Faeist philosophy of Life, Gaia's Universe and All Other Things [59] *The poem is traditionally recited every year in every village on Mayday, and every home has a copy somewhere on the premises.* [60]

When you find yourself the centre of attention,
And the need for action fully falls on you:
When you know there is no option of abstention
And you are not of the many, but the few.
You must then be the faery of decision,
By thinking of the greater good for all,
The one who makes the delicate incision,
Into the tissue full but flawed withal.
When you can carry weight upon your shoulders
Or other faery burdens on your back,
When you can scramble over life's great boulders
Without the right equipment in your pack.

---

[59] Including all the elements who didn't make it into Gaia's Universe, but remain isolated in their own – that is, of course, if such universes still exist and/or such elements still exist. Or if indeed they ever did.

[60] Though some fairy households may, unfortunately, now have to search high and low to find it, and then blow dust off it.

When you can do for others what is needed,
From instinct and without a thought for self,
See that the wider picture must be heeded
For the benefit of Pixie, Sprite or Elf.
When you can give and sacrifice your leisure,
Your privacy, security and wealth.
When you can cede your own unbridled pleasure,
In favour of another faery's health.
Then you will find the meaning of existence,
The way to inner happiness and peace:
The secret is to give up your resistance,
And watch your store of hope and joy increase.
There is no other way to be the true fae,
But to press on, though you may be scared stiff:
Be open to the promptings of each new day,
And know it must be "when" and not be "if".

PARADISE MISLAID
(Extract – in less than 12 books and 374 pages)

This prose poem was originally written some centuries ago in an ancient Fae language or, to be more precise, in Fae languages. During the more recent process of translation [61] it was noted that there were almost certainly a number of different writers, given the variations in the language used, both in terms of dialect and style, throughout the poem. Each of the Seven separate sections (Books) is itself split into 7 sub–sections (Chapters), the content of which appear to have been based upon the style and content of the Fae Chronicles themselves (see above).

It would appear that each Book may have had a different author who was well–versed in the subject matter contained within that Book [62]. Each book reflects a stage in the 'Evolution' of the Universe in general and the Earth in particular. As such there is some overlap with the Chronicles themselves, but also additional material from myths and legends of various periods of Fae history, which were all

---

[61] By some of the most famous experts of the day in the newly established ELF (Elven Language Federation)

[62] And some with their very own informal idiosyncracies.

pieced together to provide more detail of past times and also of prophetic utterances relating to the future.

The whole poem therefore consists of an overlapping series of stories that plot the trajectory of Faekind from its earliest beginnings to its future destiny. [63] The fact that so much of the prophecy contained in the final book of the poem had already come true, led most faeries to put a great deal of their trust in it to guide their future. Obviously, there will always be some that doubt, and some that are happy to let others worry about fulfilling such nonsense while pursuing their own personal dreams. But on the whole Fae communities still have an underlying belief in their legends and mythology, even if few think much about them on a day–to–day basis.

So it was that when the time came for the "Crossover" ritual to happen, it was half expected and half surprise. [64] Those that were prepared, or at least prepared to accept what was going on around them, suddenly found themselves in the middle of a climactic event, the conclusion of which would rest in their hands. The determinists in the community, however, had little time for legend and prophecy, believing that Gaia would dictate their fate. Others, the majority, pointed to the somewhat laissez–faire approach that Gaia had adopted in allowing Its Universe to develop, and took to heart the unclear ending to the poem, which appeared to offer

---

[63] Or at least the potential for its future destiny, which it held to a certain extent in its own hands.

[64] At which point deeply committed agnostics were seen to look anxiously in both directions and then sit down, close their eyes, and suck their thumbs.

optional futures depending on the response of the faeries to the circumstances that they found themselves in.

Either way, the story of the Crossover ritual played itself out, as covered in the book of the same name, and Faekind entered its post 'Paradise Mislaid' period.

BOOK THREE (EXTRACT)

Gaia looked upon Its world, the living elements
Scattered around in patterns as random
As fair–weather clouds in a summer sky;
Shapes changing and coalescing as airborne currents
Push them towards a far horizon. Vibrant colours
Merge to fashion a carpet of precious rainbow,
Dedicated to the weaver of holy pattern and rhythm.
And through the greens and blues of the providers of life,
Bursting forth with the violent force of true beauty,
The reds and yellows, oranges and purples
Provide their glorious counterpoint to the serenity
Of the wide oceans and the dense hutan. [65]

The mystery of the new is never lost on the heart
And mind of the creative force, who set
The first reactions on their path towards uniqueness;
The mutants at this stage an unknown factor,
To be revealed in later times, when surprise becomes
More to be expected, and therefore less so.
From the secure cover of the hutan canopy,
And the womb of earthly growth, emerged the Enchantment,
A joyous symbol of collaboration and harmony.
Born of Earthly matter and rooted in the ground
Beneath their feet, they move now with grace and fleetness,
Released into a world of symbiosis and empathy.

---

[65] See The Myth of the Crossover, Chapter 6, Verse 24

Weaned on the smell of damp trees and the sound of water,
The Enchanters trust their senses and live the fulness
Offered to them by faith and belief in constancy.
Not the constancy of the unchanging, but of the ordered,
Managing the flow of evolution and regulating
The direction of development – the future seen in the present.
The future a goal, a progression to be stimulated and earned,
A process whereby the future becomes another present,
And every present a stage in another future:
Stepping stones across the stream of life that flows
Through all living things, joining the two banks that together
Hold that flow in place and guarantee its destination.

And so Gaia was pleased with the forms of life
It saw created from the elements that had been drawn
Into the processes of growth and change:
Its immutability no barrier to acceptance of freedom
Of will and expression for self–created matter.
Gaia spoke, and Its language was understood
Throughout the Earth, each living form in its own voice.
"Are you all having a good time?" [66] It understood that the parental role
Of a God was one to be taken seriously at all times:
That Matter mattered, and that all was equal.
The Earthly family replied as one, recognising a unity of purpose

---

[66] Since the concept of a good time varied considerably between plants, animals, enchanters, rocks and watercourses, it is not clear what value any response that Gaia might have received would have been in practical terms. But it showed that Gaia cared.

And necessity. But Gaia saw that their voices differed,
Established and developed in separate environments
And at differing points in time during the Evolution.
The Enchanters spoke with plants and animals,
Languages born out of common origins,
And related experiences: the rocks and water
Used more ancient speech from earlier and less complex
Periods in the Creation – their feelings refined through aeons.
But from them all came back the resounding affirmation
That all was well and feelings were in unison.
Still there was a question that wormed its way into
The Gaian conscious, and lingered as the echoes died away.
From among the Enchanters came the query "What is time?"[67]
And Gaia had to think, – It had not before had a response
Of this nature, except from other Gods, and then only
With an aggressive or troublesome inclination.
This was different, and indicated a degree of curiosity,
If only from a small section of the Enchantment.

And having thought, Gaia replied. "Time is where you are
From where you were. Are is now, or at least it is where you were
When I said 'Are is now', because now is different now from what it was then.
Then is very definitely where you were, but where you were

---

[67] As opposed to "What is the time?" which is, of course, a different question entirely, but one which has become much more prevalent as time (sic) has gone on and minutiae has overwhelmed metaphysics.

Can be different depending on which 'now' it was when you asked.

Time covers all the thens and nows". And the curious Enchanters replied,

"Can you repeat that, O holy Gaia?" And they scratched their heads.

And Gaia had another long think, and said "Probably not!

But you will get the hang of it over time, and that is, in fact, an example

Of what time is! Oh, and by the way, I missed out the future,

Which is also a then, but more of a 'will be then' as opposed to a 'was then';

It is something of a grammatical nicety which you will come to love."

At which point Gaia decided it was best to end the conversation.

At the same point the Enchanters, including the curious ones,

Decided the same thing, though vowing to remain curious,

Whilst trying to work things out for themselves whenever they could.

They began by trying to work out the meaning of 'Love'. [68]

---

[68] And they are still trying.

BOOK FOUR (EXTRACT)

And the time came when the Enchanters from the hutan
Met with the Enchanters from the waters and the rocks.
They talked in the common language of the winds,
For the Enchanters of the hutan used the language of the trees,
With the rhythm of growth and the words of roots.
And the Enchanters of the waters and rocks used instead
The rhythm of erosion and the words of ebb and flow.
But the language of the winds encompassed the Earth,
and so, in this way, they committed their words to memory.
They named their surroundings and they named themselves;
They rejoiced in their similarities and they rejoiced in their differences.
The Enchanters of the hutan came to be known
As Elves, Pixies, Sprites, Brownies and Hobgoblins;
The Enchanters of the rocks and waters became known
As Gnomes, Nixies, Naiads, Kelpies and Merfolk.
And many other names were given to them, for they came
From many different environments – warm and cold,
Dry and wet, quiet and noisome, green and grey:
But they all respected each other's position
In the overarching themes of their Earthly home,
And vowed to live in harmony with all forms of matter,
For the good of the Enchantment and the support of its life.

Gaia watched as the naming went on, and on occasion

Blew the winds over them to give them the words they needed. [69]

It saw that there was a difference between each name group,

And that some of the groups were able to reproduce themselves.

The rocks could not do this, though they could become as dust,

As wind and water blew and washed over them.

The waters returned over and over to the same places

From whence they came, and flowed in a relentless cycle.

But the trees and plants, the animals, birds and fishes,

And even the Enchanters, could create more of the same.

Gaia saw that they needed two to create another one or more,

And that there were subtle differences between those two. [70]

These manifested themselves

Gaia needed names to differentiate between the two,

And so, It threw out a sound far into the ether,

Which reverberated and came back to It as "Male".

Thus Gaia called one of the 'subtleties' Male and other Female. [71]

And Gaia wondered at the complexity of the Earth;

About how the elements had been able to combine

---

[69] This is clearly an elaboration of the story from the Chronicles Chapter 6, verse 24.

[70] At this point the next few lines of the original text became blurred and indistinct as if someone had tried to erase it. It is speculated that this may be the first recorded instance of censorship.

[71] Why Gaia decided that the other term should be "Female", no-one knows. The most accepted current theory blames an untimely sneeze.

In so many strange and wonderful ways. The ability to reproduce

Was of great interest and Gaia believed this to be

A sign that many parts of the creation were of Itself. [72]

These parts have from thenceforth been known as "Orgaianic"[73]

After the naming, the Enchanters returned to whence they had come.

From Its seat in the firmament, [74] Gaia traced the progress

Of the unrooted orgaianic matter, over and through

The rocks, water and hutan to their various resting places.

But the urge to move and travel remained with the Enchanters.

The growing understanding of 'otherness' captured them

And drove their minds and imaginations to places and things

Beyond their homes, past familiarity and security.

They now lived in and with the wind that had given them

A new language and a means of learning. [75]

The plants and trees of the hutan gave them food,

---

[72] Insofar as they had choices and complex abilities to change and develop. But not the reproductive bit itself, of course, since a God certainly wouldn't want lots of other little gods getting under its metaphorical feet.

[73] This may be down to a mistranslation, since other earlier source texts have Gaia stating that such matter was "A bit like me – or 'Gaianic'"

[74] Since it is highly unlikely that Gods get tired (which is, in any case, a function of time – and we won't go there again, thank you), it is presumed that this reference is metaphorical.

[75] And also a double-entendre that has provided much entertainment throughout the generations.

And medicines for the times when they ate the wrong things,[76]

And shelter and beauty and wonderment and knowledge.

The water was theirs to drink and it gave the hutan

The ability to grow; the rocks provided tools for some,

Shelter for others, and sacrificial soil for growth.

Some Enchanters lived beneath the roots, amongst the soil and rock,

And in the darkness they created homes, seldom seeing light.

They dug through the roots of the hutan above, and formed caves

Within the loam, sand and clay; and they would enter the very rock itself

Were it not too hard for their hands or for tools made from the trees.

But fate played its part and crashing clouds with lightning bolts

Set fire to hutan, and so fierce was the fire indeed

That it cracked the rocks and melted the iron within the rocks.

And the Enchanters beneath the earth [77]emerged from their caves,

As the ground smouldered and smoked, and the molten iron

Glistened in the emerging sunlight. And they were filled with curiosity

And touched the glistening metal, such that they went "Ouch"

And "Bother to that" and[78] they blew on their fingers.

---

[76] Or just too much of the right things.

[77] Gnomes.

[78] Apparently a few words have been scratched here from the original text – and this may be the second recorded instance of censorship

Later, when the ground had cooled from the ensuing rain, they looked again

At the iron, which was now solid and dull. And it was very hard.

From that time, the Enchanters developed implements [79]

To help them expand their homes far into the rock,

And as they did so they discovered many more seams of metal –

Some iron, some lead, some copper, some tin,

And some small amounts of largely useless gold and silver.

These they placed in piles outside on the ground

Waiting for the next convenient juxtaposition of cloud, lightning.

And fire. The infrequent occurrences of these events

Frustrated the Enchanters, until one of them finally discovered

How to make fire [80] and the profession of metal–working began.

Before the invention of metal implements, the Enchanters

Were food gatherers, using the goodness of the hutan:

And the goodness of the hutan returned year on year,

Because the hutan was vast and the Enchanters few.

But when the underground Enchanters began to make implements,

---

[79] Reputedly by creating small channels in the rock to collect molten metal into "implement-shaped" moulds.

[80] The story, lacking any detail about how this momentous discovery was made, shows that it was clearly written by a faery folklorist and not by a scientist.

So it became possible to hunt animals and fish

And to cook them using fire and water heated by fire.[81]

Gaia, for the first time, began to exhibit concern

That one form of Its creation would cut short the life of another.

But It had not intervened thus far, and It would not start now.

It noted that all unrooted matter, eventually ceased to live,

And that some ceased to live due to violent circumstances;

Even if those were not its own making, nor indeed

Caused by the deliberate decisions and actions of others.

With these observations in the front of Its mind, Gaia allowed

The Enchanters to continue their developments,

Since the creation continued to exist in harmony,

And the Enchanters always apologised when cutting life short.

Soon, the variations in the lifestyles of the different Enchanters

Resulted in sub–groups emerging. The underground Enchanters

Showed differing characters as they evolved to adopt

Differing roles. Those that were glad to stay mostly underground,

Slept much more than the others, and were called "Kippers".

Those that ventured out only when forced against their will,

Were called the "Grumps". Those that loved the chance to see

The hutan and the sky, were called the "Happs". Those that needed coaxing

---

[81] There is probably a few centuries of development condensed into these three lines.

To leave the safety of the caves, were known as the "Oh Shys".

Some came to live chiefly above the ground and found medicines

From the hutan – these were the "Docs". Those that were badly affected

By the pollen from the hutan whenever they left the caves

Were called "Lergies", [82]and those who never seemed to know which way

Was up, or down, or in or out, were referred to as "Lowwits".

And so the underground Enchanters became split into seven tribes.

Each tribe lived alongside each other tribe, if sometimes uneasily,

Gaia was pleased that they could embrace difference,

And It decreed that thereafter seven would be a special number –

To represent harmony through division, and oneness through many.

From hopeful beginnings, often comes dismay;

The counterpoint to tribes in co–existence with general accord,

Is the growth of self–interest and narrowness of outlook.

While Enchanters on the edge of the hutan met with Enchanters

From the rocks and waters, and conversed and traded

---

[82] For reasons best known to themselves, most of them were given the name Al

And shared experiences and knowledge to mutual benefit,

There were others who stayed deep in the darkest tracts of the hutan.

These Enchanters seldom saw the light, and grew dark themselves:

Dark in temperament and dark in nature – the darkness of isolation.

And from isolation came envy, and from darkness came jealousy;

The choices were made with no duress, the freedom abused.

No faery is alone, [83] but separation is an option.

And so these Pixies became Nixies, hiding in the damp

Recesses of the hutan – the dank pools and the peaty streams,

With swirling mists and sodden mosses; all around the smell of decay

Unmitigated by the aromas of spring and the warmth of the sun.

Gaia gave choice, but this choice emerged out of resentment.

The other Enchanters made efforts to re–connect,

But there was no reciprocation, only retrenchment and anger.

No–one knew why, and no enlightenment came.

In this way, the Nixies grew in their isolation and protected their separation,

With fear and suspicion of all change that might benefit

Their erstwhile family, but threaten their own narrow way of life.

---

[83] This is claimed to be the inspiration for the poem of the same name – see page 28.

Gaia saw the growing rift within Its creation, and was sad. [84]
It heard the groanings from within the hutan, and yearned
To intervene to make things right. But it could not be so:
Evolution had taken a new turn, and Gaia knew that It had to step back
And let the Enchanters find their own way, and form their own plans.
And so they drifted further apart, the Nixies into their own small
And negative empire, and the others attempting to maintain
Their harmony with all other forms of matter, orgaianic or otherwise.

---

[84] Something of a new experience for a God, but one which helped Gaia to form more empathetic bonds with the developing matter on Its strange yet special colourful sphere.

BOOK SIX (EXTRACT)

When the time came for the humans to walk upright,

And stand tall upon their own two feet, Gaia gave them full attention.

The Enchanters had always walked tall[85] ,and had never seen themselves

As being any better or worse than other forms of matter that had

More or less legs, or roots or fins. The orgaianic beings

Had their own ways of growth and development, that suited

Their niche in the scheme of things. There was room for all –

The legless [86] worms and snakes; the quadrupeds and other multipeds;

The trees and plants, well rooted into their surroundings;

The fishes of the fresh and salt waters; the birds of the ground, hutan and sky,

With both legs and wings. And now the humans, dissatisfied

With the slouching gait of their hominid cousins, who kept their eyes

Focussed on the ground beneath, wanted better.

They wanted to stand erect and proud, and to cast their eyes

To the tops of the trees and the clouds and the sky beyond.

In this way, they deemed themselves to have made progress,

And better able to see up to Gaia in Its heavenly home. [87]

---

[85] In terms of verticality if not stature

[86] In the literal sense.

[87] For some reason, the humans had formed a belief that Gaia was remote and above. This is often given by the Enchanters as a reason

From Its heavenly home beside and around them, Gaia ached
As It saw certain humans lose touch with many of the realities
Of creation, and thus also lose touch with Itself.
Their pursuit of self–interest became allied to progress,
And superstition replaced the knowledge and emotions
Of earlier, simpler and more accurate times, so threatening
To create a new reality, far removed from that of the Enchanters,
Animals, plants, trees, and the wealth of non–orgaianic matter
Upon which their continued existence depended.

The Enchanters watched as the hominids and some humans
Continued to live in the hutan and amid the rocks,
Or in small shelters constructed on the large still waters.
They gathered food and caught fish and small animals to eat;
They produced tools and began to show the same levels
Of intelligence and imagination as the Enchanters themselves.
The humans that stood tallest and proudest counted only intellect
As a measure of worth; they failed to grasp the essential
Truths that intellect without intelligence, or fact without imagination,
Are both worthless, and that common sense is to be valued above all.
Gaia began to wonder what elemental mutations could have
Brought the more arrogant of the humans to the position

for the humans beginning the process of divorcing themselves - and
their lifestyle and their fate - from the workings of their intimate
surroundings.

That they now found themselves in. And It scratched its head.[88]

So it was that many humans began to disconnect

With their roots and with the realities of the matter around them.

They lost contact with Gaia and sought to find It again

In the most wondrous examples of creation that they could see.

Some saw Gaia in the trees and tried to commune with It

In the hutan; others saw Gaia in the mighty animals[89],

Or the fishes in the water. There were some humans

Who preferred to see Gaia outside of the orgaianic realm,

And allied themselves with the thunder and the lightning,

Or the volcanoes and earthquakes of the developing sphere.

Instead of living in communion with the creation – and so also

With its creator [90]– they believed only in their own Gods,

Which were merely integral parts of a greater whole.

Those who saw Gaia in the whole of creation were troubled

That there were so many different perspectives,

Leading to the potential for dissension and disagreement.

Dissent and disagreement led, in turn, to anger and disrespect,

Intolerance and separatism. Gaia was "beyond head–scratching".[91]

---

[88] Assuming It had a head of course. Such an action, metaphorical or otherwise is something of an occupational hazard when a God leaves things to their own devices.

[89] Although some of the more arty ones saw Gaia in the pretty and colourful animals instead.

[90] Indirectly, of course, since Gaia was a very hands-off sort of God.

[91] A term reserved for a state that is less bewilderment, more genuine distress.

With the passage of time, the humans came to notice

That there were occasions when they failed to catch fish,

Or failed to catch animals; or when fruits failed to grow;

Or when crops failed to sprout or just burnt up.

With customary arrogance, it was assumed that the cause

Rested with God.[92] For some this was the God of the Universe,

For others it was the God of that part of creation

Of immediate interest to their own interpretation of life.

Either way, they felt a need to try to get in touch

With their God to see if It would sort things out please!

Having failed for centuries, or even millennia, to understand

That their God was all around them all of the time,

They had to invent their own forms of communication

And rituals as a substitute for just being in constant communion.

When things did not work out the way they should,

It may have been that God was displeased with something[93]:

And if God was displeased, then the humans should be remorseful,

And this remorse would be displayed in the form of prayers and tears.

Very quickly Gaia came to identify which prayers and tears were genuine,

---

[92] Whichever, or whoever, this happened to be. By this time it had all got a bit messy.

[93] As it happens, Gaia was very forbearing, and if It had by any chance been displeased, then it would likely have been with the way the humans in question had abused the creation. Not that they would realise this.

And which were false, but in truth, Gaia would rather the humans

Changed their practices than grovel around in self–pity.

In any case, Gaia would not intervene, though It found the whole process

Instructive, and listened carefully to the content of prayers and supplications.

If the prayers and tears coincided with an upturn in fortunes

Then it strengthened the humans' belief in the care of their God.

If they made no difference to circumstances, or indeed made things worse,

Then it strengthened the humans' belief in the displeasure of their God.

Either way, it strengthened their belief, and generated a culture

Of 'must try harder', a culture that Gaia found both sad and endearing:

Endearing because it showed an acceptance of their dependence;

Sad because it showed that humans had learnt little about the ways of creation.

Moreover, some humans took belief in the displeasure of their God

To worrying extremes and introduced a ritual of sacrifice.

In less extreme form, this involved the sacrifice of a small animal[94],

---

[94] Which Gaia saw chiefly as a sad and unnecessary waste of a good animal but not fundamentally or worryingly dangerous.

But in more extreme cases, it involved the sacrifice of another human[95].

What Gaia found even more strange was the desire of the humans
To have an ever–growing set of rules to live by. It was as if
They could not trust each other to look after one another's interests.
Strangest of all was an apparent need to be told to avoid certain foods
On the grounds that they were considered dirty and unworthy.
Gaia said to Itself, "Hang on a minute. All the other orgaianic matter
On the sphere looks after itself in exemplary manner,
And fits in with the other matter naturally, knowing its own place
In the greater scheme of things. So who are the unworthy ones here?"
Gaia felt that the rest of creation should be a little insulted
By the suggestion that some otherwise harmless bits
Should be considered dirty or unworthy by the humans,
And resolved to keep a very close eye on human development
In the centuries and millennia that were to follow.

---

[95] More extreme in human terms. Gaia saw it chiefly as a sad and unnecessary waste of a good human but little more dangerous than that. For some reason, this practice also seemed to require the use of virgins, which may well be why some humans have placed so much emphasis on losing their virginity at the earliest opportunity.

BOOK SEVEN (EXTRACT)

Gaia said, "In the last days,[96] the humans will achieve the potential
To destroy all of the orgaianic matter, including themselves.[97]
It is their intellect that will enable this, but it need not be.
There will be humans who remain in communion with me
And with the rest of creation: some will be mocked, some will be banished,
And some will be hurt. They will be kept from power but they will not
Be silenced. Their intelligence and understanding will show
A new way, a better way; but hurdles and traps will be strewn
Across their paths, for the wealthy and powerful[98]
Will not readily gave up their status and the benefits that
Accompany it. Such cannot see that all that they have and enjoy
Comes from the rest of creation, and that without it
They are nothing." And Gaia rested for a moment, for such thoughts
Were knackering in the extreme, and It could not bear to
Entertain them for a long period. Having rested, It continued.
"While there are those who can see beyond their own self–interest

---

[96] Since no-one knew how long the Universe would last, the last days could be quite a long time. It is generally agreed that it means "getting somewhere near the end".

[97] Which could mean speeding up the "last days" quite a bit.

[98] Usually the same humans.

There is hope, and they can ensure a future for this 'Earth'.
But they will not be able to do it on their own, they will need
To join together with the Enchanters and all other matter
To bring about a change in the ways and intentions
Of those that are narrow of mind and arrogant of spirit."

Gaia mopped Its brow, for It knew the danger that the caring
And careful might become the self–satisfied and self–
gratified.
This was not to be a battle of right and wrong, but of survival.
"I do not need an army of 'holier than thou's', or even
worse,
'Holier than me's'", It proclaimed, "but of movers and
shakers,
And unselfish givers." It looked around again, and saw
That such an army existed, and might continue to exist
Until the time came for it to mobilise and set in train
The re–unification of all creation into a harmonious end–
game.
But Gaia also saw that the energy to set this in motion
Would not come from the humans, and so It had to warn
The Enchanters about the role that they would certainly have
to play.
For this It would need to communicate with them
Regarding the future, and it would need to be done soon.

At the right time,[99] Gaia breathed over the colourful sphere,

---

[99] Gaia had become pretty good at judging this by now, thanks to Its
constant surveillance

And a strong wind blew through the hutan and over the rocks
and water.

In the wind, the Enchanters and the animals heard new words
And new phrases and sentences. Some of the humans heard
these also
But few were able to decipher the messages contained therein.
The Enchanters heard these words, and kept them in
Their hearts and minds, to be passed on through generations
In prophecies, folklore and legend. And they waited and
watched
For the further signs and symbols of which Gaia had spoken.
Gaia had told them in the winds: "At a time that you do not
now know,
Signs will be revealed, and you should heed them.
You and the animals beside you must be aware of threats
To the creation – threats due to the actions of some humans.
You will need to work with the sympathetic humans
To protect this colourful sphere and the health and wealth
Of its component matter. And there will be one human
Who will become as one of you, and will cross over between
The human and the Enchanter as needs arise. This Crossover
Will set her eyes upon the beauty of the sphere and the
empathy
Between the different forms of matter, and will seek to bring
Other humans to work with you in the salvation of the Earth
And all its systems [100]". And the Enchanters shouted into the
wind:

---

[100] Later referred to as Paradise Rediscovered – once the Enchanters
had identified what Paradise was like in the first place.

"What are these signs, oh Gaia? Can you give us any clues?"[101]

"When the time comes, your prophets and seers must look

To a small, inconspicuous verdant island in a part of the sphere

That is not too hot or too cold[102], and not too wet or too dry[103].

The Crossover child will be in a human settlement that is

Not too big or too small[104], and which lies near the centre of the island.

In this settlement, there will be a family that is not very rich or very poor.[105]

There will be a mother and father who will have a baby girl,

Born with the potential to be the Crossover, but only if

Conditions are met. Within seven days of birth, the child must be clothed

In a warm garment of cloth from the human family, but made by an Enchanter.

If this is done, and the child then becomes Fae at least once before

Her seventh birthday, she will retain her status for the rest of her life.

As a Crossover child, she will be able to unite the humans

---

[101] This has been interpreted as the beginning of all subsequent quizzes and puzzles.

[102] In other words, just right!

[103] Ditto

[104] You are probably getting the picture by now.

[105] Whether this should be considered just right depends on your own personal social constructs.

With the rest of the orgaianic matter on the sphere

And harmony will be restored. She will go through many trials

And tribulations, but she will prevail, with the help of the Enchanters

And the animals of the hutan, rocks and waters.

The Enchanters were glad to hear this prophecy, yet there were many

Questions, chief among which was "Is that it?", for they were expecting

That things would be much more difficult than it sounded.

Gaia knew that It could not pretend that all would be straightforward,

And so It gave the Enchanters more words and riddles to keep them occupied

In thought and reason through the centuries that they would have to wait.

"The messenger will come from the land with a holy bird

And the continent with the horned antelope and the desert.

She will look for the place of the Crossover child and

Will find her where the signs are clear – the double egg;

The wily fox; the armoured warrier; the voice stick;

And a root vegetable, thinly sliced. But the Enchanters of that place

Must beware of the dark faeries, who will come to disrupt

And prevent the Crossover child from attaining her role."

The Enchanters replied: "That doesn't actually make things

That much clearer, oh Gaia," and they scratched their heads[106].
"Well that's all you're getting at the moment!" Gaia was firm.
It wanted the Enchanters to remain alert and try to work
things out
For themselves. Over time, in many parts of the sphere,
Wise Enchanters committed the signs to memory,
And later to written form in many languages and symbols.
And some would dedicate their lives to making sure
That no—one and nothing would allow the Crossover child
To arrive unannounced and unheralded.[107]

---

[106] A gesture clearly learnt from Gaia Itself and which later became
a universal symbol of bewilderment.
[107] And the rest, as they say, is history, the final chapter of which is
chronicled in the books of The Crossover.

APPENDIX

Human Folk song rough equivalents:

All around your hat = All around my hat
Blow the wind southerly = the same (traditional)
Droopy bunch of daisies–o = Bonny bunch of roses–o
Early one morning = the same (traditional)
Greenknees = Greensleeves
Hal's bad toe = Hal'n'Tow
Little Sir Pugh = Little Sir Hugh
Soggy Soggy Sue = Foggy foggy dew
The Royal Oak = the same (traditional)
The Whimbury Poached Egg = The Lincolnshire Poacher
Whimbury Fair = Scarborough Fair
Wild Mutton time = Wild mountain thyme

Sonnets and poems – human rough equivalents

As I did travel = much have I travelled (Keats)
A Faery's Story = A Fairy song (Shakespeare)
No Faery is alone = No man is an island (John Donne)
Spring will come = There will come soft rain (Sara Teasdale)
How shall I compare you = Shall I compare thee to a summer's day (Shakespeare)
The Hawk = Windhover (Gerald Manley Hopkins)
Whimbury Green = On Westminster Bridge (Wordsworth)
Sprites = Trees (Joyce Kilmer)
Dozy Man Baz = Ozymandias (Shelley)

Do not let the night = Do not go gentle into that good night
(Dylan Thomas)

When = If (Kipling)